Death Rattles

A novella by

Scott L. Miller

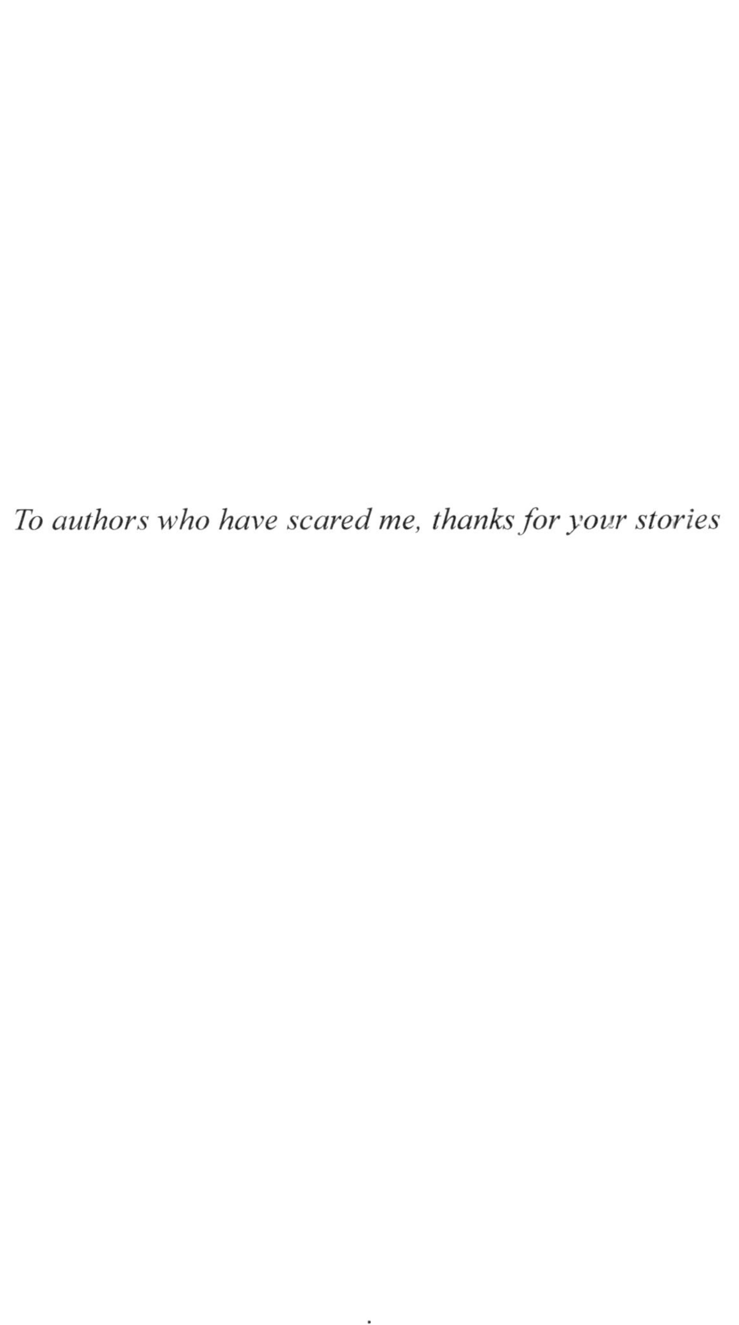

To authors who have scared me, thanks for your stories

"All that we see or seem is but a dream within a dream."

-Edgar Allan Poe

"Monsters are real. Ghosts are too. They live inside us, and sometimes they win."

-Stephen King

"Which among the colourful and crowded palette of bizarre disorders of the mind had left the ghost of a brush stroke on his brain."

-William Peter Blatty

Contents

Simple Bad Luck?

"The reason I'm here? I've come to believe it's a moral imperative that I remain alone for the rest of my life," Ashton says in a matter-of-fact manner as he crosses his legs in the captain's chair across from his therapist.

Mitchell Adams considers the various contexts of the words his new client utters to open their first session. He sees a handsome man before him of average proportions and indiscriminate age whose outward appearance is one of health and vitality. Brown hair and eyes with a white-toothed smile, a bit tanned but not overly so. He could be a clothing model for a Kohl's or Macy's catalog. "Why do you say that, Ashton?"

"Everyone calls me Ash." He smiles a bit ruefully before he adds, "It's a long story."

"We can discuss it for the next fifty minutes."

He exhales a big breath of air and shifts his weight. "We're going to need more time than that."

Mitch smiles. "Let's start with today and see how it goes."

He rubs his hands together, then tents his fingers like he's about to do the old 'here's the church here's the steeple' game for young kids. "I'm forty-two, my parents died when I was twelve in a car accident on their way to pick me up from my baseball game. I waited for hours until a lady police officer picked me up and told me the news. A spinster aunt took me in and I lived with her until she died of cancer when I was eighteen. She died at 53. I've been on my own since then."

"I'm sorry to hear that. Aside from the early deaths of your parents and aunt, how was your childhood?"

"Overall, it was a generally happy time. No siblings, but I had supportive friends. I completed high school and earned average grades. My aunt left me her small house and a nest egg. I didn't want to go to college, so I got a job at Kinko's to help pay the monthly bills. My favorite subject in school was history. I know everything about history from the time man first walked the earth. I had no legal issues and no drug or alcohol abuse aside from occasionally getting drunk on the weekends. I love to travel and can proudly say I've visited every country on the planet. Four years later, I married my girlfriend at City Hall, and life was good. We tried to get pregnant, but it turned out she was infertile, and a couple of years later, she died of a heart attack from a congenital condition she didn't know she had."

"That makes four deaths of people quite close to you. How old were you?"

"We were both 28. About three years later, I married my second wife (we met in a support group for people who'd lost their spouses at an early age, became friends, and later started to date). Six years later, she died suddenly in her sleep."

"How awful. If my math is right, you were about 37?"

He nods and says, "She was 41."

"And you're 42 now?"

Another nod. "There's more. In between marriages, I dated and fell in love with a woman who was divorced once before. She had a big house and a good-paying job.

When she died, the daughter went back to live with her father."

"How did she die?"

He stares out the floor-to-ceiling windows of the seventh-floor office. "She died from an overdose. Her close friends didn't know she was chipping (I didn't know the meaning of the term until a friend told me later what it meant). She had chronic pain from a fall while skiing and was on pain medication. The coroner said she died from Fentanyl. She bought extra pills from a friend, and they were laced with the drug. The next woman I dated I saw once, and the next time I saw her, she said she was diagnosed with breast cancer. She wanted to focus on her recovery, so we never had a second date … which was probably a good thing."

Mitch clears his throat. "What makes you believe that you somehow factored into these deaths?"

"I'm the common denominator. What other explanation is there?"

"Some people die young, in accidents or by diseases or conditions or drug abuse or heredity. Others stay alive and married for sixty, even seventy years. I think seven percent of American couples have been married at least fifty years."

He stares at the tops of his shoes. "It cannot simply be bad luck."

"Why not?"

He shrugs his shoulders. "I see death and reminders of it everywhere. At home, when I drive my car, and even when I shop. Not a minute goes by that I do not stare death in the face."

Mitch's brow furrows briefly. "I don't understand. How do you see death everywhere?"

He looks away, thinking he shouldn't answer the question truthfully. "It's hard to describe. I just do."

"Hmm, maybe we'll come back to that question later. So far, I chalk it up to simple bad luck. How do you feel when this fear of death overcomes you?"

"It feels like I'm having a heart attack or a bad panic attack. High blood pressure and anxiety, during which I'm unable to catch my breath. I feel a rush of impending doom, and my palms get sweaty. It feels like the room, and the world spins faster and faster until it's out of control. I'm tired of it all, and I don't want to get accustomed to it. Now I feel if I'm attracted to someone and I pursue them, they will die."

Mitch thinks: *Everyone we meet will eventually disappoint us, because everyone dies*. Mitch waits a beat while his client takes a sip of water. "Did you feel this way when you met your wives?"

He nods. "I was excited each time I met a new person, then scared that meeting me would start their dying process. That feeling of dread has been exacerbated with each passing year. I have no luck with women, I guess you'd say."

For the rest of the questions for that hour, Mitch's initial working diagnosis is thanatophobia, or death anxiety, a specific and existential phobia in which the triggering situation is getting close to another person.

His feelings of fear, panic, and anxiety are difficult to control and manage, but they haven't prevented him from leaving his home. Mitch doubts he will be able to see his new client for long unless the diagnosis is incorrect.

Ash agrees to a second session next week. He likes the positive feelings he received from the therapist and the no-nonsense approach he seems to use. He holds out faint hope that this therapist somehow may be the one to actually help him, even though he kept things from him. Big, important things.

His last client before the weekend lingers outside the Sevens Building with nothing to do the rest of the day until he sees Mitch exit the front door from a distance and, on a whim, decides to follow. Mitch makes a series of turns until he reaches CJ Mugg's, a restaurant in Clayton. At the entrance, he meets an attractive young brunette, kisses her, and they walk inside holding hands. They are seated at a table along the windows. He waits ten minutes and walks in, takes a seat at the bar where he sits facing Mitch's back and can watch and listen to them from a relatively safe distance.

Ash orders a beer and, from the corner of his eye, assesses the brunette. She has a lean, athletic build, is slightly shorter than Mitch, and radiates a warm smile. She wears a professional-looking pants outfit and some tasteful obsidian jewelry that compliments her bob-tousled hair with subtle highlights. He feels an instant liking toward her, and she reminds him of a taller, more substantial version of the actress Mila Kunis. The woman intrigues him and he wishes he could somehow touch her. Their waitress brings her a glass of white wine and Mitch a beer. They order salads, she a Cobb and he one with smoked salmon. He only hears snippets of conversation due to the increasing noise near the bar, but when he observes people, he often sees colors that arise from the conversations, and he sees only the warmest shades of blue, green, and violet rise from their table. On other occasions, he can sometimes predict fights before they begin when bright reds, purples, and blacks arise over the people he's watching like cartoon thought bubbles. It sounds like she had a busy day at work with her boss, but he can't quite discern what she does for a living. Before their food arrives, Mitch gets up to use the restroom, so he buries his head in a menu to hide his face.

The barmaid asks Ash what he'd like to eat. He's not hungry, but he orders a basket of fries to appease her.

During their meal, Ash can't hear much of the conversation, but he hears that they have tickets to something at The Fox tomorrow but can't make out if it's a concert or a show. They seem like the happiest of couples; warm greens and blues continue to emanate above their table. They order a second drink, so Ash orders another beer. By now, the noise becomes impossible to hear their conversation, so he takes a hundred from his wallet and leaves it for the waitress after eating one French-fry and downing a beer and a half. He leaves the restaurant and walks up the street opposite the window where the couple sits.

At home, he looks up Mitchell Adams on his computer, makes several phone calls to associates, and eventually learns his address and phone number. He was always good with computers and knew the best and the worst people. Mitch does not have a Facebook profile, so there is nothing there to learn about his social life or possibly hers. He wishes he knew the woman's name, as she intrigues him in many ways. He feels a stirring inside. He tells himself to fight this feeling, but biology almost always wins in these instances with Ash. He goes to sleep with her face and body in his thoughts.

A Riot and Living in a Burning House

Elijah sits on his ramshackle front porch, a glass of cold, fresh-squeezed lemonade in his hands, while a friend plays a soft, airy tune behind him on the guitar. Through the ragged elm trees, a full moon shines down. He turns to his friends King and Moses and says, "What we got here with this car coming toward us, Mose?"

Moses looks beyond the heads of neighbors passing by on the street. He stops rocking on the porch swing. "Who all's in that T?"

King puts down his guitar and squints. "Hard to tell. They look white."

A black Ford Model T rumbles down the rutted road through the black area of town on a hot summer night. The light is fading, and the air is electric and still. The car slows down, and two white male passengers fire multiple shots into the group of blacks on the street and speed away. Moses and King are hit and fall dead in the melee. The shots appear random. A bullet passes through Elijah's shoulder as he screams for the women to stay inside the home. His neighbors attend to him and the other fallen victims. Five people are dead in the street and two on Elijah's stoop.

In his mind's eye, the streets fill with sharp flashes of reds, blacks, and deep oranges once the shots are fired. The colors entangle and mix into various fusions of those shades as the people who can run for cover. His eyes flutter beneath his lids, and his blood pressure spikes.

An hour later, he watches a neighbor get Elijah to a doctor, and then a similar Ford containing four other white people, two of them cops, pass through the same area. Friends of Elijah, Moses, and King, thinking this to be the same car that started the shooting frenzy, open fire on the car. The bullet-riddled car escapes with two dead cops in the back seat.

The sleeping man watches this gruesome nightmare transpire in his mind's eye while he naps in his single bed. His eyes continue to move rapidly from side to side beneath his eyelids that do not open. His lips purse in anticipation.

He looks over the town, which is a rough industrial and manufacturing city that contained more saloons than churches and schools that year in 1917 and was home to about 10,000 black Americans out of 60,000 residents.

The next morning, he watches as thousands of white men gather to view the cops' bloodstained car, and it doesn't take much effort to work themselves into a frenzy. Nothing but reds and blacks hover above them when they come to an agreement that there's only one thing to be done. Friends and co-workers of the dead cops arm themselves with every weapon they can find and storm into the black section of town. They beat and shot black people indiscriminately, women and children included. The vengeful mob cuts the fire department water hoses before they torch the black sections of town. Then, they shoot the blacks when they run to escape the flames.

The sleeping man stirs in his bed and whets his lips. A faraway, curious half-smile plays on his face, but still, his eyes remain closed.

For the next two days, he watches as blacks are massacred at Broadway and Fourth solely because of the color of their skin. Elijah was lynched when he tried to prevent his wife, Mame, and their two young children from being shot. Hundreds of blacks fled across the Eads Bridge into St. Louis to escape the violence, while another 1500 sought refuge in city buildings. The Illinois National Guard was ordered in on day three of the riot, but the Guard initially joined in on the attacks on blacks. A black cloud of death hung over the city, and the air was still and close. Young white daughters of the two dead cops brandished clubs and chased black women through the streets to beat them to death. The riotous mob attacked photographers and destroyed their cameras, so very few pictures survived the obscene carnage of that week while city police harassed journalists who considered covering the events. The police chief estimated a hundred blacks had been killed, which is likely an underestimate, while eight whites were confirmed dead. Six thousand blacks were left homeless after their homes were burned. Months later, the state charged 25 blacks and 10 whites on charges related to the massacre.

The man's eyes open wide. As before, he smells fear and sulfur and blood in the bedroom. He walks to the bathroom to throw water on his face. His body tingles, and the hairs on his neck stand as he thinks of the terror of the gruesome events that played out before him. What he doesn't recall is stopping near the border of East St. Louis and Belleville for lunch earlier that day. When he paid the bill, the fingers of the half-black, half-Vietnamese waitress touched his. He doesn't know why he has an erection, but it's happened before, and it slowly recedes.

He drifts off to sleep again.

It's June 10th, 1963, in his dream, and a crowd of 350 monks and nuns dressed in long white robes pray and march slowly through downtown Saigon. They stop on the road outside the Cambodian embassy. A blue car pulls up, and a monk exits to place a cushion in the center of the road. A monk named Quang Duc also exits, sits on the cushion, and assumes the lotus position while other monks and nuns encircle him.

He notices the calm and strangely subdued colors of greens and blues and purples swirl above the heads of the people in the street, even the man on the pillow. The colors begin to spin and become light yellow and orange.

He watches a third monk exit the car with a white five-gallon container and pour liquid over the seated man, who rotates a string of wooden rosary beads and says, "Nam mo A Di Da Phat" (an homage to Amitabha Buddha) before he strikes a match and drops it on himself. His robes go up in flames before his flesh burns and turns black, as oily smoke emanates from his burning body.

He inhales the singular acrid and coppery smell of burning flesh that fills the street. Once you smell it, you never forget it.

Quang Duc feels every burn over his entire body while he does not deviate from the lotus position, the epitome of self-control. He does not make a noise.

He feels the unimaginable and unbearable pain of the monk, but somehow, Quang Duc remains subdued and, on the pillow, the entire time. It must have taken an unbelievable amount of self-control. His skin turns black and splits open to expose the lower tissue beneath the skin to the flames, but he doesn't choke on smoke and soot. His muscles seize in agony. The superheated air around him makes it almost impossible to breathe. The sick smell of burning human organs and boiling blood fills the intersection, and the crowd learns firsthand that human beings burn surprisingly quickly. Ten minutes of excruciating agony later, Quang Duc is dead. Spectators watch his body slowly wither and shrivel up; his bald head blackens and chars. Witnesses swear he never moved a muscle, never uttered a sound, and remained outwardly composed until, at last, his lifeless body fell backward. Shortly before the self-immolation, fellow monks lay their bodies down in front of and behind the tires of the local fire truck to ensure Quang Duc would not be rescued. Most of the spectators stood in stunned silence, but some eventually began to wail and pray. Others prostrated themselves before the burning monk, even the policemen, who had orders to control the gathered crowd.

The man's eyes flicker underneath his closed lids and he displays night sweats. His body slowly rolls to the right and then left as he watches with envy the controlled discipline of the monk and his fellow believers.

When the fire is out, a group of monks covers the body with yellow robes, pick it up, and try to place it in a coffin, but the burned legs can't be straightened, and an arm protrudes from the box before it is carried to a nearby pagoda.

Back in America, he listens as President Kennedy comments that no prior picture in history has ever generated so much emotion around the world as the famous picture of Quang Duc sitting calmly in the lotus position while on fire. Buddhist practitioners indicate this was not a form of suicide, nor was it an extreme form of protest against the Vietnam War.

A Buddhist monk spokesperson said later that Quang Duc took the "Bodhisattva vow," in which he vowed not to liberate himself from suffering before all other beings are also liberated. By setting himself on fire, he hopes to awaken those who don't recognize that they, too, are living in a burning house and must find their own way to quench those flames or to escape.

The monks concur that Quang Duc burned with compassion for the suffering of all life.

The sleeping man wakes and rubs a hand over his face and arms, expecting to feel destroyed skin. His alarm goes off, and it's time to start a new day. That was one of the most intense and realistic dreams he'd ever experienced. Emotions fill him. It is only then he remembers the brief interaction he had with the waitress at lunch.

Bright Lights and Roses

That Saturday, Claire Kelly felt excited and a bit nervous. She smiles as she sits on a plain wooden stool, tuning a guitar, a single white spotlight on her. She wears black jeans, boots, and a white embroidered blouse. She looks out at a small but packed house. She sees the dark silhouettes of waitresses who carry trays of drinks to people she can't see who sit around tables she knows are there but can't quite see as smoke rises through the thin shaft of light toward the ceiling. On the stool next to her is a plastic bottle of water and behind her stand her backup singers Lorraine and Toni.

The applause recedes as she leans forward to speak into the mic. "Thank you! For my next set, I'd like to offer some of my favorite older songs. Ones that I believe have superb lyrics, all written by different artists. Lorraine and Toni are going to sit this one out. The first one comes from 1975 and speaks of a relationship and why it was destined to end. I wish I'd written the words, but a very talented woman did, whose voice remains great, though it's deeper now at age 83. She was born in Staten Island, and the song is about her relationship with another famous folk singer/songwriter."

A male voice in the crowd calls out the writer's name and someone else the name of the song.

She shifts her body so the guitar faces closer to the mic. She repeats the beginning Em chord on the guitar several times while she says, "Kudos to you both!" Then the guitar is the lone sound on stage until her voice sings the opening line, "Well, I'll be damned, here comes your ghost again ..."

Cheers rise and quickly fall as she continues the lyrics in her three-octave range soprano voice. The words seem haunting, exactly the mood the songwriter wanted to convey. At the song's end, the cheers return, and she swivels her head to the side to wipe a tear from her face. The set is going well. Claire is a visceral performer; her moods adapt to that of the intended ones for the lyrics. The cathartic release is one of the reasons she loves singing and performing.

"Thank you! For the next song, I need to return to the piano, and this one's a singalong to brighten the mood ..."

At the end of the hour, she receives bouquets of roses and a standing ovation. Her set ends at 10:30 after she does two encore songs that the audience requested. The owner is pleased, and after she pays her backup singers, she secures her guitars, mics, sheet music, and other equipment in her electric car. She returns inside to eat a light complimentary dinner with her man. The bouquets have been placed in glass vases at her table as centerpieces.

Mitch Adams leans over to kiss her. He smiles and says, "You were amazing! Joan Baez would have been proud of *Diamonds and Rust,* and you knocked *Hallelujah* out of the park for the final encore! Plus, you look fantastic."

Claire has changed into a little black dress and a pearl necklace. She nods and says, "Thanks for being here and for all the flowers." She leans closer to add, "I'd rather go to our favorite restaurant to celebrate, but I didn't want to turn down the owner's offer. I haven't been doing this for long, and I don't want to ruffle any feathers."

"I only sent you one bouquet of roses—"

She notices a person standing at their table. "Just a second, Mitch." She makes eye contact with another diner.

The college-aged woman says, "Excuse me. I just wanted to say you were great! I'm a music student at SLU. Could I have your autograph?"

Mitch loans her his pen and she asks the fan's name. She personalizes it and signs the woman's copy of the flyer announcing Claire's concert tonight. "Thank you! You know what, Susan? This is my first autograph."

Claire hands back the autograph and they thank one another. "Good luck in your studies."

"One of many autographs to follow," Mitch says after the young woman leaves. "Well deserved."

They share an appetizer and a bottle of chardonnay as neither wants to eat a heavy meal this late at night.

Her cell rings. "Hi, Arty. Yes, I think it went well, too."

She listens for several minutes. "That's great! I will get back to you with a decision. 'Bye."

She turns to Mitch and grabs his arm. "That was my manager. A record producer expressed interest in my demo tape, and the assistant manager at The Pageant saw my set last week and wants me to play as an emergency opening act this Friday for the group Kimberly Q. That means there will be a brief review in the Post the next day about my music. This is all happening so fast!"

"Great! It's all a potential foot in the door. I'm proud of you!"

"The Pageant! I'm not sure I'm ready for that big a venue. Arty expects me to accept and wants to meet with me this Wednesday to talk about making a record!"

"This is the break you've been looking for, hon. You have a great voice and talent!"

They clink glasses when the bar owner interrupts to thank her for the show tonight. He hands her an envelope and says, "A good crowd tonight! You want to play here again, let me know, and I will find a spot for you."

Claire invites Mitch back to her Clayton apartment, where they relax in the cool night air on her balcony before they make love in her bedroom.

In the morning, they shower and walk to breakfast at First Watch. Her cell rings again, and Arty wants to meet with her in an hour. She kisses Mitch at his car before she returns to her apartment. Above the car, the colors are the same warm greens and blues as before.

Neither notices the nondescript man standing across the street pretending to stare inside the storefront of a local business. He watches them part in the reflection of the glass window; forbidden thoughts swirl in his mind. The cloud above him is dark and blackening.

Trouble in Paradise and War

The sleeping man observes the following in a dream.

The man in his dream looks at his girlfriend like she's insane after he loads his SUV. "Why don't you just leave me alone?"

She frowns and folds her arms across her chest. "All you want to do is go to Vegas and gamble and drink. We don't have sex anymore. It's like your mind's a million miles away. This isn't working for me."

He shrugs his shoulders as he turns back to the garage. "Do what you gotta do. I'm gonna do what I gotta do." He rubs his eyes, feeling sharp pain behind them. "At this point, it doesn't matter anymore."

He can read the man's thoughts while he watches him pull out of the driveway: I'm 64 years old, have been divorced twice, got no kids, but I'll be damned if I allow a long-term girlfriend to talk to me like this. My old man was a bank robber, but I didn't follow his path. The only run-ins I had with the law were traffic tickets. I made good money in real estate that let me retire comfortably in the retirement center I chose. I've earned whatever lifestyle that I want.

He watches the man drive 80 miles southwest to Paradise, Nevada. He sees and experiences the black rage of his shadowy thoughts in the SUV the entire trip that washes over his body in waves. At the hotel, the concierge remembers the balding man with the mustache and partial beard and checks Stephen into a room on the 32nd floor of the hotel on September 25th; bellmen carry five suitcases to his room, another seven bags the next day, two more on the 28ᵗʰ, six suitcases on the 30ᵗʰ, and two more on October 1. Four days after check-in, he also pays for a second, adjoining room. He's a familiar figure to casino hosts in Las Vegas because he's a high-stakes gambler who's stayed there many times before, earning complementary rooms and meals. He stays to himself mostly, playing video poker machines while drinking heavily. His gambling luck has soured over the last two years, losing a significant amount of his wealth, but during this stay, he makes sure to pay off all the gambling debts he's accumulated. He laughs when he considers this act a noble one, given his plans. He was never a moocher or thief and doesn't want to be remembered as one. During this week, he makes multiple return trips to his retirement community in Mesquite, where his girl-friend continues to rag on him about their relationship. He doesn't care, for it's about to end.

Back in his hotel room on October 1, he placed *do not disturb* signs on the doors to both suites and screwed an L-shaped bracket into the door and door frame of his room. He uses a hammer to break two of the windows in both of his suites. In the suites are twenty-four firearms. There's a black cloud shrouding his brain as he begins to shoot into the music festival crowd at 10 pm. In ten minutes, he fires over a thousand rifle rounds from rifles on bipods and from ones with bump stocks. He doesn't remember aiming after the shooting starts. Something takes over in him, and it's like he's on autopilot. He feels an invisible but weighty hand on his shoulder guiding his actions. This is his destiny, what everything that's happened in his life until now has led up to.

The sleeping man watches the chaotic action unfold in his mind's eye as his attention shifts to the street below and the terrified, fleeing rabble. The crowd for the country music festival is trapped inside a fenced-in area for minutes. Most bleat like sheep as they stumble over themselves in a steel pen, awaiting the finality of the abattoir.

Panicked concertgoers initially mistook the repetitive noise for fireworks until those around them started to fall dead or were wounded. A stampede follows, but the survivors are initially trapped in the concrete lot by the security fence. He experiences the last minutes of their lives and the abject terror of the others being trapped, awaiting their time to be executed. Most of the thousands of fans escape, but hundreds do not.

Then he watches the man on the 32nd floor shoot eight bullets at a large jet fuel tank at McCarron airport 2000 feet away. One bullet penetrates the tank, and Stephen grins, expecting a gargantuan explosion, but he doesn't know that jet fuel is mostly kerosene and unlikely to explode. He'd hoped that explosion would bring even more terror and maximum carnage; at least, that's what the unseen figure with his clawlike hand on his shoulder whispered to him.

The shooting is over after a mere ten minutes, which felt like hours. By then, police had located the source of the shots, and at 11:20 pm, they breached the two suites with explosives and found the shooter dead from a self-inflicted gunshot wound to the head. No way was he going to let them take him alive. They find no note from the shooter and learn of no motive for the bloody massacre.

Sixty people died, 413 were wounded, and another 454 were injured trying to escape during those frenzied ten minutes. The police later find ammonium nitrate, over fifty pounds of explosives, and 1600 more rounds of ammunition in his SUV.

The sleeping man's brown eyes snap open, and a warm fuzzy feeling overcomes him. He smiles and puts his hand in his underwear and feels a stickiness inside. His body tingles with post-coital excitement.

While the sleeping man ate dinner at a restaurant earlier that night, he watched a program at the bar showing a no-limit hold 'em tournament in Las Vegas at a casino close to the one that became known for the infamous mass shooting.

He can't fall back to sleep yet, so he turns on his bedroom television.

He drifts back to sleep with the *History Channel* playing their holocaust series, and the screen shows an SS official looming over a concentration camp member near a large chamber. As the announcer grimly and dispassionately describes several of the primary experiments, the sleeping man inserts himself into what isn't recorded on the film as he watches a Nazi doctor place a Dachau prisoner into a low-pressure chamber to simulate the conditions their pilots would face when forced to eject at high-altitude. He doesn't mean or even want to do this; it just happens, at least that's what he tells himself. The doctor monitors their physiological responses as they succumb and die. The man in the white coat at times dissects the subject's brains while they are still alive to search for the tiny air bubbles in the blood vessels of the brain. Those who didn't die in the chamber or on the operating table were summarily executed. The man in bed experiences the helpless terror of the subjects and feels the cold calculation and superiority of the doctor as he performs the tasks with no second thoughts or remorse. If he were brutally honest with himself, he'd admit he enjoys the feelings of condescension and dominance over this captive group of diminished people. The purpose of the next experiment he watches with his eyes closed is done for the benefit of the German army when they suffer gangrene. The Ravensbruck camp doctors inflict battlefield-like wounds on prisoners and then infect the wounds with streptococcus, tetanus, or gas gangrene. The man feels the anguish of the prisoners when the doctor aggravates the infection further by rubbing ground glass or wood shavings into their wounds or by tying off blood vessels to simulate an actual wound in battle. Many subjects died from the trauma.

The sleeping man's reveries break when his alarm goes off in the morning. He's turned a corner tonight. He feels rested and refreshed. The small part of him that used to feel bad for having this power has been subjugated by the feelings of strength and control it provides.

"You didn't list any insurance on your intake paperwork. Do you have a provider I can bill on your behalf?" Mitch asks his new client.

Ash settles into his chair across from the therapist. "I don't have insurance. Just bill me."

Mitch allows the silence to build.

"I was lucky enough to win the lottery two years ago."

What he fails to say is he's won six different major state lotteries as an adult, far exceeding the prior record of two. When he gets low on money, he partakes in an old Indian tradition called a sweat in some tribes. It's not a real sweat, but his closest approximation of one. He goes to an isolated area on a hot summer day and strips naked except for a loin cloth. He remains baking in the sun until he passes out from exposure, exhaustion, and dehydration. The first time he did this, his mind was so cleared of the world when he woke up that a set of six numbers appeared before him. He wondered what the meaning of it could be, for the numbers stayed with him the rest of the day. On a whim, he played the numbers in the next day's drawings and won six million dollars. The effort exerts a major toll on him—severe sunburn, high fever, intense headaches for days, and his electrolytes get dangerously low to the point he requires IV fluids. It takes him a week to recover. A small price to pay for not having to worry about money for years. He tried it again soon, but the numbers never came to him. Years later, it worked five more times, but only when he was destitute, with no money in his bank account. Both sets of grandparents were said to be clairvoyants in the old country, and they made a living off their abilities until they arrived in America. He never knew their specific capabilities until years later, after he touched an old family black-and-white photo. It was so painful he vowed never to think of them again.

"Good for you. Did you play certain numbers?"

Ash squirms briefly and shrugs. He represses a smile. "I think I just pulled them out of my head. Blind, dumb luck."

"I was wondering, in our first session, you said you've visited every country on the planet. Is that true?"

He nods. "Like I said, I love history and have the money." He laughs self-consciously.

"So you've visited all 195 countries?"

More nervous laughter and a nod. "That includes North Korea, Eritrea, Libya, Iran, Yemen, Turkmenistan, and others. Even the poorest, most backward countries have fascinating and unique places to visit and interesting people to meet." Passports from other nationalities helped pave his way into the difficult countries and he spent thousands of dollars to keep himself safe in unfriendly countries. Some countries restricted his travel to specialized and supervised group tours, and the real threat of kidnapping caused him to spend thousands on security, but he kept this to himself.

"That boggles my mind. You must be one of a very small number of people who can make this claim."

"I guess so."

He wants these sessions to continue and takes a deep breath and exhales before he continues. "I almost didn't keep my appointment today. My anxiety and fears have gradually increased and prevented my ability to travel. The past two months, more days than not, I can't find the strength to leave the house. There's a constriction in my chest that makes it difficult to breathe. It grows until I reach the point where I think I'm going to die."

After pointed questions and feedback from Dr. Adams, he receives homework prior to their next session for him to identify every symptom related to his panic, what triggers the symptoms, and what makes them worse. Listening to the therapist, he almost believes that this focused CBT will teach him to gain control over the agoraphobic symptoms he just invented.

Now Mitch has the needed diagnosis to keep the sessions going. His diagnosis shifts from thanatophobia to debilitating panic attacks.

Something Old, Something New

Mitch picks up his new silver Chevy Camaro convertible at the dealers after trading in his old, reliable red convertible Solstice. He'd ordered it months ago with all the desired bells and whistles after realizing it was time to make the change. His old Solstice is no longer being made and parts were getting hard to find. It was an emotional time to hand over the keys. The car had seen him through challenging and dangerous cases; it had been vandalized, rebuilt, and been with him through several relationships with women. He considered a more environmentally friendly car, but Claire has an electric car, and he decided to postpone the inevitable switch for one more fun ride.

Claire's is his next stop, and she meets him outside her apartment in a yellow summer dress, sandals, and a matching floppy summer hat.

"Very sexy," she says, touching the side of the car with a finger and flinching as if the contact burned her skin. "I love the shiny color. It looks better than the pictures. Is it as fast as it looks?"

He revs the engine to create a throaty growl. "Why don't we find out?"

She holds onto her hat when he gooses the engine on Highway 40 westbound, and the car shifts gears. "Oh, my!" She looks at him and cracks a smile. He places his hand on her thigh and laughs because that's her bedroom line when she's getting close.

They park at the home developer's office to review and discuss blueprints of the modern home they are building together in a new development called Stonegate Meadows. The oversized lot is at the end of a cul-de-sac and backs to a wooded lake with a southern exposure. Plenty of glass ceilings in the two-story home with a sloping roof, a second-floor covered deck, and a fenced upper courtyard. Inside is an open and airy floor plan that seamlessly connects the living spaces.

They meet with Derek to discuss their plans, and Claire starts by pointing to a list of options. "I decided on these sound panels for the bedroom that we're converting to a studio and the speakers, positioned here, which means this wall needs most of the outlets," she points to the far wall.

"Excellent, that makes sense," Derek says while he makes notes.

Mitch says, "I decided I want a private entrance for clients after all, and I'd like it here, along the side of the home next to the garage, if it's not too late. I want a panic button here, near where my desk will go. He insists on this after last year when a client attempted to kill him, and the panic room in his Clayton office saved his life. We don't think it detracts much from the backyard ambiance, especially with the future trellis going in to separate the living space from the client entry."

Derek nods. "I can cut a door frame there. No problem."

For the rest of the time, they debate and choose fixtures for the three-and-a-half bathrooms, the top-of-the-line appliances for the heart of the home, which is the chef's kitchen, colors for the sleek countertops, and the style and color of cabinets and pulls. They choose a soaking tub and jacuzzi for the master bath with a separate shower and dual vanities. The other bedrooms offer built-in bookshelves, and the smallest one will serve as Mitch's client room. The final discussion today involves choosing slate stones for the gazebo area. They finish by visiting lot 6, where construction continues. The Tyvek commercial home wrap is now affixed on the outside walls, and the grading has been mostly completed; the double-paned windows have been installed.

Derek says if the weather remains good, the rest of the inside and outside work could be done in three months' time. They lunch at Manno's, their favorite restaurant, where they drink extra dry Tanqueray martinis and share a rack of lamb and Chilean sea bass. They are celebrating the progress on their new home, her new singing gig, and what may be her first record contract. She decides she will play The Pageant Friday and needs to write three more original songs for her CD.

They share a slice of chocolate cake and then walk to his new car. Mitch asks her to fish his sunglasses from the glove compartment. She finds nothing but a gold box.

"That's it," he says.

"There aren't sunglasses in here." She opens the box and gasps.

His breath catches, and he gets down on one knee. "I love you, Claire. Will you marry me?" He never imagined he'd do this. He always believed the idea of proposing in a restaurant with the ring in a glass of champagne was overdone and cheesy. As he ages, his thoughts on marriage have softened. He knows he's ready with Claire.

She puts a hand over her mouth and tears well. "Oh, Mitch! I never thought this day would come. Yes, I will!"

They kiss and hug. He places the ring on her finger, and she says, "It's beautiful!"

Later, in the car, she says, "Why didn't you ask me at the restaurant?"

He shrugs. "It's already an emotional, pressure-packed question. I think it should be asked in private."

"Did your parents know your plan?"

He nods as he starts the engine.

Claire redoes her makeup in the rearview. "I have to give her credit; your mother didn't let on during lunch yesterday."

"How were the games?"

"We took two of three sets on the court. She moves well for her age and covers both sides of the court. She cleaned my clock at chess after lunch, but she's a good teacher."

"How about we stop and see them? Dad has a bottle of champagne on ice that he's been ready to pop for decades and I'm sure mom wants to inspect the ring and make sure I chose well."

Her seat belt fastens with a click. "So, Dad will be happy you're at last getting married?"

"He thinks marriage will somehow make it less likely I take on dangerous clients in the future. One has nothing to do with the other. It's not like I seek them out. Sometimes, the danger is in their families, and the dangerous ones have found me twice. My days of seeing dangerous clients should drop to nothing.”

Claire insists they stop and buy his mom flowers.

They pull into the driveway of a small two-bedroom home in West County. His parents downsized to this house because it’s easier to clean and maintain now that it’s just the two of them. A string of white balloons attached to their mailbox flutters next to a congratulations sign.

“Were they that confident I would say yes?”

“I texted them your reply when we stopped for the bouquet.”

Mitch’s dad, Alan, still works part-time as an emeritus accounting professor at Gateway University, and his mom, Jean, taught English before she retired a generation ago. His dad opens the door. Average height and thin, his hair is brown and his beard is graying. His mom joins him at the door and waves. Her pixie-style haircut frames her face well. They both are tanned and have great smiles. They play golf together while Alan likes to fish and Jean plays tennis.

Dad points to his wife, Jean, as Mitch and Claire walk to the door. “The balloons were her idea.”

Claire and Jean hug before she hands her mother-in-law to be the flowers. Alan hugs Mitch and pats him on the back repeatedly. “Good job, son! You’ve got a winner with this girl!”

Jean says, “I’m so happy for both of you! Come in!”

The four sit in the living room while they recap the proposal and share the latest news of the home building. The nearby lake is already stocked with fish and Alan smiles at that. He excuses himself to pop the champagne and bring glasses.

After Alan makes a toast, he asks if they've thought about a honeymoon destination.

Claire looks to Mitch and shrugs her shoulders, "I've always wanted to visit Paris."

Mitch drains his glass and looks at his mom. "We haven't set a wedding date, but Paris in the spring sounds great. Did she tell you her singing career may be taking off? Her manager thinks she's ready to cut her first CD once she writes a few more original songs. She's working on fine-tuning and perfecting the songs. She also has an offer to open at a major local music venue. We'd like to wait until we know more about her career before we set a date."

After further discussion of his proposal, Alan returns the subject to Lot 6. When Mitch mentions they are turning the smallest bedroom into an office/client room, Alan looks down at the carpet. "I thought you'd keep the clients in the office since you installed that special room." He pauses and adds, "One never knows what stressed, imbalanced people may do, not even you, son, and they'd be inside your new home with Claire."

"Those were aberrations that Claire knows all about."

He hides the disappointment from his son, but he shivers.

"The murderer and Blaze?"

"Even them."

Had anyone looked outside the front windows right then, they would have seen an average-looking brown car slow down, with an average-looking male in the front seat staring at the home. He parks on the opposite side of the street. The space over his head is absent of color.

Something Stolen, Something Blue

Standing in front of the bathroom mirror, Mitch puts the finishing touches on a half-Windsor knot to a dark purple tie and grabs the coat of his black suit. He looks at himself a final time before he calls over his shoulder, "You about ready, hon?"

Claire appears in the doorway in a lavender Midi-dress, sans shoes, and smiles. "Five minutes to fix my hair. You look nice."

A somber Mitch types the address into his phone, then watches his fiancé brush her hair and fasten the straps to her shoes.

They drive to North County and enter Bellefontaine Cemetery. They pass the Busch Mausoleum and settle in behind a line of cars. He follows the signs to the designated parking area. They walk a gentle rise to an area shaded by a large white canopy where two coffins sit atop their rollers and mourners gather. A breeze lessens the heat of the noonday sun on this cloudless day. He hears the bass voice of JoJo Baker, a black city homicide detective, and turns his way. They shake hands, and Mitch hugs the tall, slender woman next to him and offers condolences to both.

"What happened, JoJo?" Mitch eventually asks.

Baker steers him away from the women, and his voice cracks. "Drunk driver, broad damn daylight. He crossed the center line in a head-on crash. The bastard left the scene and hasn't been caught. Cops are looking for the car, which was still drivable by some sick miracle. The car was registered to a priest and was reported stolen from the rectory parking lot the day before. Simone's dad was driving LaKeesha to the doctor." He glances at Simone, who cries out with joy and hugs Claire after she notices the engagement ring. They jump up and down with contained excitement, given they're in a cemetery.

Baker shakes his head. "The crash killed him instantly; LaKeesha died in the ambulance on the way to the hospital."

"I'm so sorry. That is awful. How do you know the driver was inebriated?"

"Witnesses saw him driving erratic as hell. He drove up on a sidewalk and wiped out a table setting in front of a restaurant. The man did a lot of damage on the block. No description other than he was white."

An elderly tiny woman wearing a Dashiki and a purple turban approaches Baker for a hug. She's hunchbacked, and the anguish in her voice brings mixed memories to Mitch from a decade ago.

"Mitch Adams, you remember Skinny Yolanda. Skinny, Dr. Adams."

Those kind brown eyes look up at his face and light up. "I remember, you're the man who helped Lonnie before he was murdered."

"Miss Yolanda, you and your son taught me as much as I helped him. I'm so sorry for your losses."

She nods. "You can pay your respects to him while you are here."

I turn to Baker, who says, "I arranged for Lonnie's remains to be transferred here years ago so he could be next to Earl, along with others from our family. They're in the row above the open graves."

A decade earlier, Baker asked Mitch for a favor, to see a disabled man in city jail accused of counterfeiting. Lonnie was a slight man with a bad club foot. Mitch didn't know it at the time, but Lonnie and Baker were half-brothers, and LaKeesha was Lonnie's mentally challenged mother. Lonnie was guilty as charged, but he gave away every perfect counterfeit bill that he printed to the deserving poor in his neighborhood. The chief prosecutor in St. Louis at the time had his underlings hunt down the counterfeiters and did his best to find the remaining bills. He planned to fund his next political campaign with phony millions. Lonnie died brutally in jail, but Mitch helped the police catch the prosecutor, who was arrested along with his henchmen. Mitch came close to being killed by the prosecutor's goons once he learned of his plan but escaped with minor injuries.

Mitch pays his respects to others in the family, especially Shirley Sparks and Tyra. Little Ty is also present, one of the boys Mitch paid to guard his car back then, but DeAndre died at a young age from a drug overdose.

Baker shakes his hand after he learns of their engagement. "I never thought you'd get hitched, my man."

Mitch shrugs. "Never say never. What about you and Simone?"

"Not you, too? Yolanda's been nagging me for years. She says if I don't make her an honest woman before she dies, she's gonna come back and haunt me the rest of my days."

Mitch laughs. "You don't want that, trust me."

He glances her way and laughs nervously. "Word."

Simone and Mitch hug, and he offers condolences while she congratulates him on the engagement.

After the service, Mitch visits the graves of Lonnie and Earl Washington. He places a rock on top of Lonnie's tombstone in remembrance of the gifts people dropped on his coffin before it was lowered a decade ago. The memories from then threaten to seize him when footsteps approach from behind. He turns to see Baker carry Skinny, then stands her down next to him.

"Lonnie was one of the best people I ever met," Mitch tells her.

She nods. "He thought well of you, too. It was part tragedy the way his story ended, but you made sure he didn't die for nothing. You helped him carry out his last wishes as much as could be done."

"I don't know about that, but thank you."

A blue jay lands on a nearby branch and squawks before flying away. She turns to face him. "Your fiancé is a fine young woman. Give me your hands."

He hesitates because he remembers when she asked to grab his hands ten years ago. She foresaw his future. Unlike the first time, she doesn't arch her back as much due to her advanced age and osteoporosis, but she frowns and her eyes close before she sways on her feet. He considers breaking contact with her, fearing her next prescient words, but he worries she may fall, and besides, it's too late. "A black cloud follows you. I can't see through it. Like me, it's a pre-cog but is many generations older. I can't see what it wants, but it's very bad. Eject this evil from your life before it causes you unspeakable agony." Her eyes open wide, and a look of terror fills her face. She reaches up to touch his cheek. "Remember these words."

Mitch wonders what Yolanda was referring to when she referred to the black cloud as *it.* And what does she mean when she says pre-cog? He's about to ask when her eyes roll back.

Before Skinny falls to the ground, Baker scoops her up in his strong arms. Skinny passes out from the effort, like she did ten years ago. Baker turns to Mitch and lowers his voice, "She blames herself for the deaths. She was supposed to drive LaKeesha to the doctor that day instead of Simone's father, but she had a really bad flu and couldn't get out of bed. She would have gladly taken his place in that car. She hasn't been herself since. The cloud she spoke to you of may have been following her; I'm not sure. I gotta get her home. This affects her so much more now; she'll be in bed for days. That and she's more … erratic since you saw her last. Thanks for coming, Breezy; it means a lot to us."

Breezy or Cool Breeze are nicknames Baker had for me once we became friends after he tried to arrest me for murder a decade ago.

The average man parks the damaged blue Range Rover with stolen plates in a city parking lot. He replaces the CLERGY sign on the front dashboard with a smile and walks away. He was lucky it still ran, but that's why he chose this particularly large and heavy model. Some people glance at the damaged car, but few pay him close attention, and no one asks if he's okay. It's time to flee the scene. An older homeless man turns from his shopping cart, stares at his damaged car, and is the only person who eyeballs him for some time. He washes his face and hands in a nearby public bathroom and tosses the stolen car keys in the trash can. He texts for an Uber on his phone app and gives the driver an address within reasonable walking distance of his house. His right knee throbs from the impact, but he can walk home. Stealing the car was an easy thrill, one he'd mastered years ago. When he first grabbed the wheel, the memories that rushed up his arms into his chest and the feelings associated with them were so severe and intense he had to pause before he could safely drive away. The number of budding, young lives and their families that were changed forever by the clandestine events that happened in the back seat of this car boggled his mind. He fought the ruinous memories here, but frenzied feelings of domination and control and lust still broke through his consciousness. At times like this, he thought his powers were a curse. If the police had his special abilities, no criminal could ever get away and every cold case could be resolved, but the last thing he wanted to be was a cop. He decided how he wanted to use his gifts a long time ago and had no regrets. He followed in the footsteps of his nomadic family.

Pain had shot into his knee when the airbag engulfed his face. He longed to get out of the Rover and touch the man in the car, but he couldn't run the risk of being caught. He punctures the deployed airbag with an ice pick, backs up, and finds the car still drivable, though the damaged grill scrapes a front tire and begins to smoke. During his walk home after the Uber ride, he recalls the look on the face of the male driver he killed. It changed from concern to anxiety to dread in an instant. The man screamed upon impact and called out a woman's name ... Simone! He watched the light in the man's eyes go out, and he was dead. Was that the name of the woman in the front passenger seat or someone else? Once home, he chews five aspirin and puts ice on his knee. He closes his eyes and remembers a small part of him thought it would've been okay if he also would have died in the crash.

In an earlier moment of quiet reflection, he'd decided to see Mitchell Adams again because of intense feelings of loneliness and isolation. At times, he despises his special powers. He longs to be a normal person but doesn't know how, especially with his abilities that can take control of him at any time. Like his parents, he's a prisoner to his supernatural powers, a freak of nature and humanity, adrift in a world of normality.

Before his father became a butcher, he walked the downtown streets with an organ and a monkey. Happy, upbeat music filled the streets while his mother worked the crowd as well, selling lavender while she carried around baby Ash in a papoose and begged for money for milk. His father could look at an animal and know what it was thinking and anticipate its actions before the animal itself knew what it would do. He trained the frenetic monkey to run among the crowd and pick pockets and was never caught. Mother also conducted seances and fortune readings. She was a master manipulator of the human condition, able to read someone's history within a minute or two of meeting them. Once the townsfolk learned of their subtle cons and the police intervened, the father found a job as an apprentice butcher, and the mother raised baby Ash at home.

An Old Sepia Picture

One night, he puts contemporary music on in the background and cracks open a beer after he had half a bottle of wine with dinner. On the TV tray next to him is a late-night snack of cheeses, grapes, and crackers. In his lap is a book of ancient knowledge, the family album he created from the old country.

He puts his feet on a hassock and dons a pair of disposable plastic gloves. He does this because every time he handled the album in the past, heat seemed to emanate from it, and the big book seemed to quiver on its own. He has a healthy respect for and belief in the evil eye. He runs a hand over the rough-sewn cover of the large book he acquired from a village elder during his travels. It seems every color of thread that comprises the spectrum of hues is part of the cover, and several wider threads hang down for use as bookmarks. He opens it for the second time since he assembled it. The first pages contain hand-written letters in the Balkan language from his parents and his grandparents, the first of his family to sail to America. He reads the translations of them all and harkens back to his travels.

The next page contains antique daguerreotype photos from the 1840s of Romani female ancestors dressed in what he assumes are multi-colored dresses (given the fact that the sepia tones around the subject are the only vague color in the photo), some with large sashes and fringes, posing in front of their huts while a whispery trail of smoke rises between them. He frowns and stares at the pictures; an uneasy feeling washes over him that he can't place at first. Then it hits him. He thinks the two women have somehow moved within the picture since the last time he looked at it, that their faces have turned and now glare at him. He slams the book shut and closes his eyes until his blood pressure slows. He thinks he may be losing his mind.

Years ago, he used Ancestry.com to track down his more distant family of origin movements and then visited Spain, Bosnia, and Hungary, where the people he met told him what they could remember of his earlier nomadic relatives who moved in and out of their regions or hooked him up with others who claimed to have first-hand knowledge. He acquired the contents of the book during his many journeys across Europe and knew this was but a small percentage of his family roots. The oldest man in one village he met seemed shocked when he heard his old-country family name and spoke in a tremulous voice of the powers his forerunners wielded and nurtured. When he asked the man for specifics, he performed the sign of the cross and left without a word. He walked all the nearby villages, where the people still stage flamenco and perform belly dances for money. Many more donations led him to hire Romani translators, which led him to obtain the album cover and the arcane pictures within, with multiple tall tales told at times around fireplaces deep in the woods, many too bizarre for him to believe. The reactions of the elder natives he sat down with were mostly curiosity or fear. Occasionally, older adults wore a look of sadness. One drunken street urchin said the early history of his family that was handed down orally sounded like myths and folklore or the stuff of legends. The raspy old urchin remembers his great-great grandfather recounting the tale of all his ancestors being run out of town on a rail for practicing magic and witchcraft. The family routinely received the evil eye each time they were exiled from a village. Many of the same villagers who forced his family to pack up and leave suffered the same horrible, suppurating illness and died painful deaths. This resurrected tales from them of the Bubonic Plague many centuries earlier, for which the Romanis were blamed. The survivors quietly blamed his ancestors for the deaths. Nomadic Romanis were often made into slaves, and some European countries forced sterilization on them. In past times, these people were referred to as gypsies. The word itself has now fallen beyond the unsavory category of political incorrectness to unacceptable use in polite society.

He opens the book again and studies the pictures. He tells himself he must be mistaken. The women are in the same pose as before. He studies the sedate pictures of his parents and reads letters from his father and mother; both encourage him to follow his heart and find his passion. His father urged him to use his gift wisely and never abuse it, though he was unsure how they wanted him to do that since he recalls his parents using their gifts for their own self-serving needs.

The music ends, and before he rises, he looks at the daguerreotypes. His face turns white, and he throws the book down, which upends the TV tray and spills the snacks onto the carpet. He looks around the dark living room repeatedly before he rushes to the kitchen and throws salt over his left shoulder. He hears no sounds in the house until the raucous music of strings, pan flute, and cimbalom come from the radio station in the living room. That music has never been on his radio station before tonight! He runs to his bedroom and locks the door. He removes the gun from his nightstand and puts it under his pillow. The only thing he knows to do is to try to fall asleep and ride out this storm.

For the next four hours, he focuses on sounds in the quiet house. The daguerreotype picture showed only the huts and smoke rising from the campfire. The old women were gone!

He dreams he's back in an old rural Hungarian village where the tiny houses have straw huts. The sky, everything around him, has a sepia cast to it. Suddenly, he hears the tinny sound of small cymbals clanging nearby behind him. Turning, he sees a woman dressed as a veiled belly dancer smile lasciviously and walk away from him, her ample hips gyrating to the music as she rounds the corner. She looks like one of the belly dancers he met during one of his trips. It begins to pour rain, and a woman calls out in pain, screaming for his help. He follows the sound to a cliff, for the cries are coming from down below. He hears a twig break behind him, and when he turns, the two old relatives from the old daguerreotype picture push him off the cliff. They spit at him while his legs flail in the air. He falls and falls until he wakes up in a sweat in his bed, his index finger wrapped around the trigger of his handgun.

In the morning, he searches the house; the doors remain locked and the windows closed; the only thing he doesn't remember is picking up the fallen cheeses and crackers from last night. The TV tray has been put up and folded away in its place.

"Thanks for seeing me on short notice," Ash tells Mitch as he rubs his hands together.

"You're welcome. How can I help?"

He looks out from the seventh-floor picture window and clears his throat. "I think I may be losing my mind."

"What makes you think that?"

"Last night, I could have sworn I saw things that weren't there, or rather, things that should have been there but somehow weren't, which would mean either I'm going nuts or every physical law in the world is meaningless."

"What did you see?"

Ash laughs and shifts in the chair. "Oh boy, you're going to think I am losing it! After dinner last night, I looked at a family album, and the women in the picture were no longer there. The background remained the same, but these old relatives I never knew were … gone."

"Are you sure you were looking at the right picture and not a similar one, minus the people?"

He nods.

"Are these relatives alive? What is your relationship to them?"

He doesn't say they made their living doing stereotypic gypsy endeavors or readings. "They're part of my European family tree. I've never met them, but their names were Anna and Stella, and they never strayed from Hungary. They were old in the 1840s. They have to be long dead."

"Has anything like this happened to you before?"

He pauses. "I don't think so."

"What did you feel when this happened?"

"At first, I thought it was real. That they'd somehow left the album and were coming to hurt me. Then I felt fear, and my skin crawled. I don't know them; they don't know me. I felt disoriented and certain I was losing it." He keeps to himself what he did next and exactly what these relatives did for a living. He doesn't mention any special powers. He tells Mitch of the dream he had.

"Is there any meaning you can attach to this?"

A much longer pause this time. He shakes his head. "No. Have I lost my mind?"

After some time, Mitch replies, "Did you have anything to drink with dinner?"

"Half a bottle of wine, then a beer, but I don't think I was intoxicated, and I don't do other drugs."

"Did you look at the album again, and were the relatives back in the picture?"

He hangs his head in shame. "I did not. I woke up late and had to get ready to come here." He fails to say he was too afraid to do so. When he returns home, he will search everywhere inside to make sure nothing is untoward with the gun he left in his car. He considers burning the album or throwing it in the Dumpster but wonders if there would be repercussions like a curse if he angered the dead from his family tree. He wishes he could ask people from the old country what he should do next.

Mitch asks him many questions about whether he's had other odd experiences he can't ignore, heard voices others can't hear, or heard voices, clicking or ringing sounds in his ears, and whether familiar surroundings look strange or threatening to him. He denies all and says he has no knowledge of family members with a history of psychosis.

"Has something changed in your life, for the good or bad?"

Ash looks away. He thinks: *what's new are the feelings I'm having for your girlfriend.* A smirk appears on his face but disappears when he faces his therapist. "I met a woman."

Mitch smiles. "That's good. Tell me about her."

"I haven't met her yet. With my unique *problem*, I scout a potential woman to see if I'd like to be with her and then decide if I should take the risk. For her sake and mine."

A puzzled look comes over Mitch. "How can you make that decision without talking to her and seeing if you may be compatible?"

If you only knew my superpowers. "It's difficult, for sure. It takes time. It's a feeling that comes over me."

"What do you know about her?"

Ash stalls for time by pretending to retie a shoelace. He wasn't expecting this turn in the conversation and must think quickly. "She's beautiful. She has a great smile and laugh. She appears independent, and she's not married. She has a career and seems to be a really nice person."

An alarm sounds on Mitch's watch. "What does she do for a living?"

"She's ... in the entertainment/service industry."

"Good for you! The only way to find out is to meet her. Our time is about up for today. I'd like you to accomplish two tasks before our next meeting. The first is to make notes if any of these unusual visual disturbances recur and write down what you were doing, thinking, and feeling at the time. It may even be helpful to start a diary if you don't have one already."

"Okay. What's the second thing?"

"Introduce yourself to this lady you're attracted to. Talk with her, maybe ask her out for coffee. See if you might have things in common."

Ash thinks: *I know what we have in common; it's you.*

He feels a rush of excitement and says sheepishly, "I think I could do that."

Mitch stands. "Until next time. Have a good weekend."

A Frustrated Building Inspector

Claire drives her parents to Lot 6 for the first time after picking them up from the airport. Claire wears cowboy boots and jeans as the dirt front yard remains wet from last night's rain. Alan and Jean follow her on the temporary walkway of boards into the frame of the house. She describes what the rooms will be. Jean likes the modern style with the odd-sloping roof and the large modern gas fireplace with the front and left blaze. Alan is more traditional with his home preferences but keeps that to himself.

"The foundation inspection passed with flying colors. Over here will be my studio in this soundproofed room, and the electronic system will be along this wall."

"Looks like the HVAC system and rough plumbing will be added next," Alan says, noting the equipment stacked on the floor as he inspects the craftsmanship and occasionally nods his head. The windows are in the installation process, and he approves the quality of the double panes. "Looks like the structure has good bones, Claire Bear."

Claire hugs her dad. She loves that he still sometimes calls her by her childhood nickname. It connotes happy memories.

"When will the roof be installed?" Jean asks.

"After the plumbing and wiring are installed and inspected, honey," Alan answers. "There's an established order to building a house."

"We're going to meet with Derek next week to make the final decisions on fixtures, kitchen cabinets, hardwood floors, and appliances."

A shuffle of feet behind causes them to turn. An average-looking man with a bushy mustache in a hard hat holds a clipboard and walks through the rough frame of the first floor. He notices the warm greens and blues over her head. He stares at Claire the entire time and only notices her parents when he walks up to her.

Jean breaks the silence. "Hello, are you Derek?"

The man looks at her and back at Claire. "No, no. I'm one of the site inspectors."

Alan steps forward. "I have a few questions …"

The man puts a hand between them and shields himself with the clipboard. "I'm sorry, sir, but I'm looking for the owner Claire."

She steps forward. "That's me."

He offers his hand and smiles broadly. "It's a pleasure to meet you. I want to congratulate you because this is going to be one beautiful home with a great view of the lake."

He shifts the clipboard to under an arm, and their hands touch. He wraps his other hand below hers. His eyes close. After an awkward pause, Claire breaks off the contact and says, "Hi, have I seen you before?"

He sways, eyes still closed.

"Buddy, are you alright?" Alan says to the man, supporting him to make sure he doesn't fall.

His eyes pop open, and he stares at the concerned threesome. "I think I need to sit down."

Alan directs him to the steps, where he gingerly sits down. The man puts his head in his hands. "I think my blood sugar must be low."

"I know what that's like. I have some cookies in the glove compartment. Can you get them for him, Alan?" Jean says.

Alan hustles off to the parking lot. Before he returns, the average-looking man collects himself and rushes from the shell of the house the other way down the block. Claire calls to him, but he ignores her as he sprints to his car.

His hands shake as he fumbles for the keys. Once inside, he hunkers down in the seat and makes sure no one has followed him.

When Alan returns with the cookies, he's surprised the man is gone. "Where'd he go? Do you know who he is?"

Claire shakes her head. "I've never seen him here, but I think I've seen him somewhere before. I can't place him."

Alan picks up the clipboard the man dropped. "I know one thing: that man is no building inspector." The pages clipped in it are blank and he shows it to Claire before he drops it to the floor.

After they finish their tour of the new structure, Claire stops by the contractor's trailer to see Derek. She describes the man with the clipboard who claimed to be an inspector.

"Was he wearing a name badge?"

Claire looks at her parents, and they all agree. "No, he wore a generic yellow hard hat with no logo on the front. He has a very bushy mustache."

He frowns. "That doesn't sound like any of the guys I know. Let me know if he shows up again."

Alan asks his building questions, and ten minutes later, the three leave.

Claire tells Mitch that night of the strange encounter with the man, but he also doesn't recall seeing a mustachioed man of that description on the job site.

The average-looking man needs ten minutes before he is physically able to drive. He throws the fake bushy mustache from the car. The images he received from their contact were the most intense he's felt in his life. An ocean of greens and blues filled his soul, from her childhood through her adult years, or what he assumed to be his soul. No early trauma, she loved and enjoyed school, she and her parents have a great relationship, she's in the best of health, and he picked up on no adult losses or dysfunction aside from a few breakups with boyfriends. She loves to sing and write songs and hopes to make that her new career. She loves Mitch like she's never loved another person.

She's beautiful and personable and nice. She's in perfect health.

She's one in a billion, perfect, save for one flaw—she's in love with his therapist and plans to move into a new home they're building together.

Dark browns and blacks fill the car, which forces him to roll down the window so he can breathe easier. His heart races for five more minutes. There are ways out of this.

Forget her.

Move on. Walk away. You told your therapist you believed you should be alone for the rest of your life. You even babbled something about a moral imperative to do so.

She's the most baggage-free woman he's ever met. She smiled at him. Her touch was beyond electric. Shivers coursed through his body that forced him to close his eyes again. He had no idea how long or how weird he must have seemed to the three people, standing there like a crazy man clinging to her hand. Whatever, the ice has been broken. They could be together, and they could work.

If *he* was out of the picture.

Could he drive a wedge between them, and if so, how? Paying another woman to sleep with him and photograph the indiscretion? Would he succumb? How much time would that take? Would it even happen? Would it drive her away from him? That's too hard to control. He could assassinate his character in other ways ...

No, he must be gone from the picture completely.

Ash would then enter her life as a supportive friend, and she would come to see him in a whole new light, for now, he knew beyond a shadow of a doubt they were meant to be together.

He slept that night with a pen he'd pocketed from Claire when she sat briefly on the stair riser next to him. He placed it in the front pocket of his pajamas. Once asleep, he floated in through her open bedroom window while a light breeze swayed the diaphanous curtains. He stared at her, sleeping in nothing but a long T-shirt; as she moaned and rolled over to her other side, the T rode up and exposed more of her long, tanned legs. He noted a birthmark high above her right knee. Excited, he moved the sheet back, and as he prepared to climb into bed with her … the spell was broken, and he woke with a start in his own bed.

He looked around. The pen wasn't in his pocket anymore or in the sheets, or on the bed, or on the carpet. He turned on the bedside lamp and reached for the gun in his nightstand. He checked under the bed, in his closet, unlocked his bedroom door, and slowly made sure the doors and windows were locked; he turned on every light until he reached the album on the kitchen table. He'd placed a heavy book on top of it, just in case. He hadn't checked the picture since his last session with Mitch. He moved slowly, like he was a bomb defuser, and turned the pages to the pictures, and the daguerreotype picture showed only the huts, cooking fire, and rising smoke. He slammed the album closed and looked around the room, unsure what to do.

He looked under the mattress, turned the bedroom upside down, and then the entire house. Where could the damn pen have gone? He was furious the first joyful reverie with Claire he'd waited so long far had been interrupted. He had no true north to turn to, no family to ask how he should respond. He tried to return to Claire's bedroom in his mind, but he couldn't without the physical touch of the pen. He was alone, this man of impressive powers and ability, but he felt helpless as a baby stranded in the deepest of woods. He needed something else of hers.

For the rest of the night, he had to be satisfied with memories of her past he'd gleaned from shaking her hand.

A Sweetheart, a Wolf Call, and a Baba

Mitch settles down in the front row with his best friend Tony and his wife Cindy and their drinks. The four have double-dated twice, but this will be Claire's first concert his friends have attended. Claire is tonight's opening act for a female group of national renown whose stop in St. Louis is part of a worldwide tour. The group's usual opening act had to be canceled tonight due to a lingering illness of their singer. Claire was delighted to hear the offer from her manager and agreed to the opportunity to fill in on short notice. The money was good, but more important was the chance to play in a much larger venue at The Pageant in Clayton. It was an exciting step up.

She walks on stage fifteen minutes late at the stage manager's request due to the late-arriving crowd, which happens sometimes in this town. She wears her trademark black jeans and a white shirt with dark blue stitching on her shoulders. Two days ago, she had her bobbed hair trimmed and the highlights redone. She carries an acoustic guitar while much of the crowd still arrives to find their seats. Her backup singers take their places behind her. The guitarist and bass player are new to Claire, courtesy of her manager, and they've played together less than a week, but she feels like she has her own band now. Mitch senses she has some nerves as she sits down on a stool to tune the guitar and adjust the mic to her height. The crowd buzzes when the lights flash and then dim.

She stands and clears her throat before she walks along the front of the stage to acknowledge the arriving audience and waves to the crowd in the second deck. "Good evening, St. Louis! I'm Claire Kelly, a local singer. I know many of you were expecting The Hummingbird Girls, but Melanie, their lead singer, came down with a throat infection, so I will be the opening act for Kimberly Q tonight."

Mitch and Tony cheer her on. A man in his thirties with his arm around a girl several seats to Mitch's left shouts *Alright, baby! Let's see what ya got,* emits a wolf whistle and flashes her a thumbs-up.

She notices the man who whistles at her before she begins, then nods and playfully crosses her eyes at me, which tells Mitch her nerves will be fine. She plays A major chords until she sings the opening lyrics to Tracy Chapman's *Fast Car.* She receives mild applause at the song's end. "Thank you! The song is not about a fast car but rather details the struggles of a young woman to break free of being one of the working poor. This next one is by one of my favorite female artists, a Brit with a London cockney accent, and it goes like this ..." She starts to play in the key of Cm and is a simple song to play on the guitar, at least Claire told me it is. The applause grows after she and her backup singers finish Adele's Rolling in the Deep. She walks around the front of the stage and waves to the audience. "The title refers to a UK slang that means a person always has your back, but in this break-up song, it turns out not to be true for Adele, and she basically tells the guy to buzz off." Claire plays Bleeding Love by Leona Lewis, White Rabbit by Jefferson Airplane, and her current favorite, Diamonds and Rust, by Joan

Baez. The patrons are now all seated, and the cheering grows. Claire continues to share tidbits with the audience about each song. After the Baez song, she introduces her backup singers, who take a bow, then Jeff, the new guitarist, and Rob, the bass player. She takes a sip of water, and during the brief silence, the wolf whistler in the front row calls out, "You have any original music, sweetheart?"

"Who said that?" Claire shields her eyes from the spotlights to look his way and asks the crew for the house lights.

"You, sir?"

The man, with his arms crossed, nods.

Claire speaks into the mic so the balcony and the entire house can understand what's going on. "A gentleman in the front row asked if I have any original music, which is a good question. I want everyone to know I'm writing songs for my debut CD. For those who may want to follow me, you may visit my website: clairesings.com. Thank you very much for the question, sir, but that said, please don't call women you don't know 'sweetheart, honey, or baby.' It's patronizing, and you're old enough to know that."

The women in the audience cheer; even the woman sitting next to the man playfully swat his shoulder. He shrugs, reluctantly nods his head, and claps with the rest of the audience.

Claire puts down her guitar and walks to the baby grand piano. Her second set starts with her version of Crucify by Tori Amos and continues with an energized variation of Because the Night by Patti Smith. The crowd is feeling it, and she immediately segues to You Make Loving Fun by Fleetwood Mac. She points in the direction of Mitch and smiles while she harmonizes with her back-up singers. "That was for Mitch in the front row! I'm going to end tonight with one of my favorite Carly Simon songs …"

She hears the audience call out: Anticipation; You're So Vain, among others.

"Nope," she says and plays a lengthy piano solo before she sings the lyrics to Jesse.

Claire finishes and points to her backup singers and musicians. "Thank you, St. Louis! Please give it up for the powerful voice of Toni Simpson and the smooth silkiness of Kathy Gaylord, the enigmatic Jeff Brown on guitar, and wild man Rob McMann on bass. She claps for them all while they take a bow. They share high-fives. Claire approaches the front of the stage with her singers, and Mitch hands her a bouquet of roses and a single rose for Toni and Kathy. The audience stands and cheers for minutes, even the wolf whistler.

Mitch tells Tony and Cindy they've been invited to her dressing room during the intermission while the stagehands change the set for the main act. The lights turn on over the seating area. The wolf whistler gives a thumbs-up to Mitch as they make their way to the dressing room.

They hug backstage. Cindy and Tony are blown away by her voice and musicality. Claire removes her make-up and changes into a fresh pair of clothes. On their way out, they pass the group Kimberly Q, four costumed women with spiked hair and outrageous outfits, and Claire tells them to have a good show.

They celebrate at Manno's restaurant in Chesterfield. After a toast, Claire says, "The manager of The Pageant wasn't pleased with my interaction with the loudmouth. He chided me for it, but he understood why I said what I did. He said I needed to lose the rabbit ears when on stage as the customer was almost always right. He said there's a reason the Lilith Fair ended more than a decade ago. "That comment pissed me off, and then he said do you know that radio channels only play a select number of songs by women each hour, even with the popularity of Taylor Swift?"

"I thought the guy was condescending. I wonder what his date thought of him," Cindy says.

"He was being a pompous dick," Tony offers in his silky-smooth voice.

"I understand where the manager is coming from, but the heckler accepted what you had to say. In my opinion, you handled it well. It was a win-win," Mitch says.

Claire sits down at their table and says, "Sadly, the manager's right. Women remain minorities in the music industry."

We each order separate dinners and sample. I love their sea bass in white sauce, and Claire had the rigatoni Ubriaco while Tony ordered the rack of lamb and Cindy the veal Milanese. We share a Caprese salad, and Claire says, "A strange thing happened today at the house site. I drove my parents there, and a man in a hard hat entered and asked for me. We shook hands, and he must have had some kind of fainting spell, I guess. He said it was low blood sugar, so dad went to the car because mom had cookies there, but by the time he returned with them, the man stood and hurried away. I had no idea what he wanted."

"Had you seen him there before?" I ask.

She shakes her head. "No company logo on his hard hat or shirt, and no name badge. The guy said he was a building inspector, but dad didn't think so because the guy left his clipboard and all the pages were blank. I saw Derek later, and he couldn't place the man, either."

"What'd he look like?" I ask.

"He had a bushy brown mustache; no other distinctive features come to mind."

"Did he have an accent? Did he get into a truck or a car?"

She seems surprised by my interest. "I don't think so. He ran down the hill, turned a corner, and was gone. I didn't see any vehicle. Why all the questions?"

Mitch dialed it down a notch. "It's weird. I was trying to see if I could recognize him from the site, I guess."

Cindy sips her wine. "That sounds a bit odd, especially since he ran away like that. So, if he wasn't an inspector, why was he there? Was he being creepy?"

Our dinners arrive when Claire hunches her shoulders. Mitch raises his dirty martini. "To my future wife and future rock/contemporary music singing star.

Congratulations on completing the next step along the way to your exciting new career!”

She shares something she now learned from her agent via a text message, that a date has been set during Thanksgiving week to record her first CD. “So, between now and then, I need to write at least three more original songs. My first deadline!” They raise their glasses again.

The man outside pulls a Cardinal ballcap over his eyes and enters Manno’s long enough to catch a glimpse of the foursome. He wishes he could touch something of hers again but decides to leave the restaurant. Mitch drove them here in his new Camaro, so touching his car would be pointless. They close the place down, and no one notices the generic brown car that follows them at a safe distance on the drive to Mitchell’s townhouse.

His sleep is restless, and he finds himself alone in a rural setting, following a path that winds through woods heavy with the aroma of mulch, leaves, and other decomposing objects until he arrives in a tiny rural village of thatched huts where chickens pick at the ground, and untethered goats munch grass. This bucolic section is far from the usual charming pastel-colored houses and rolling hills Hungary is known for, but it’s quaint. Low clouds scud across the sky. To the left of the track is a fenced garden with a scarecrow dressed in peasant garb. The scent of manure follows him until it mixes with smoke, and he freezes at what he sees beyond the well.

It's not just any old fire. It's *the* fire, but no women stand in front of it. No one is visible in the tiny village. For some reason, he's not afraid and walks up to the bubbling cauldron over the fire and finds what looks to be goulash. The dish smells fantastic; it looks like the last thing it needs is a large dollop of sour cream. He stirs the concoction, and the heat warms his face. He recalls how good the comfort food in Hungary tastes and that their outdoor cooking is unparalleled. He's starving and looks for a bowl, but there is none around. But assumes he can find one in the huts.

A horse whinnies over the hill when noise comes from the huts. He takes a tentative step toward the nearest one when an old peasant woman with a long, hooked nose and a scarf covering her head steps out of the hut. She is heavy-set and hunchbacked and uses a thick wooden cane carved with animal figures. She was the long-lost relative on the right-hand side of the picture. When she sees him, an obscene leer plays across her wide face, and she emits a loud cackle. He turns and runs away from her down the path. When he looks behind him, he's amazed by what he sees. The old crow of a woman is levitating over the ground and gaining rapidly on him, cackling all the while. How is this possible? He veers off the path and into the woods he'd passed earlier, certain she'd be less able to follow him due to the growth of trees, but still, she gains on him. He finds the cause of the earlier mulchy smell as he sees the woods contain the rotting carcasses of animals, small and large. He didn't think the bones were here before. He looks behind once more and trips over a root, falling to the soft ground. He lands next to the decomposing skeleton of a human. When he turns, the old woman stands on the ground and wields a knife over him. "This old Roma and her sister need meat for our next stew. You will do, little Baba. Nice and plump!"

When the knife slashes at his neck, he rolls away from her and sits up in his own bed in a sweat. He clutches at his throat, which is free of blood. He feels as if his heart is there, and it takes ten minutes of deep breathing to calm himself. He closes his eyes until his breathing normalizes. The dream felt so real. He thinks: *am I losing my mind? Have these reprobate gypsy hags somehow left my family album and are coming to kill me? Did I just travel into the old daguerreotype picture to be accosted by one of them? What am I going to do? What can I do?*

He stands to get a glass of water and feels something on his head. He removes a dried leaf from his hair and looks at it in amazement. In the bathroom mirror, he sees streaks of mud and what looks like decomposed matter on his pajamas. Panicked, he brings his gun into the bathroom, throws his soiled pajamas in the trash, and showers. He walks to the kitchen with the gun and slowly opens the family album. To his relief, the two women in the daguerreotype picture are right where they should be, and everything looks normal. He studies their faces and the one on the right looks exactly like the cackling woman in his dream. He goes to bed and tries to wrap his mind around recent events. If this is a dream, did I unconsciously sleepwalk outside and wake up back in my bed? The person he most wants to talk with about this is Mitch, but he can't.

The Center Cannot Hold

Marty, Claire's manager, arranges for her and her makeshift band to cut a few singles in town, so Claire drives from her Clayton apartment to downtown and parks at Muddy Rivers Producers. This is to gauge the local level of interest in her new music prior to the recording of the CD. Marty is working to get her to be an opening act for certain shows at a new venue in Chesterfield called The Factory. She's been practicing her new songs at local studios and here at Muddy Rivers.

She's been writing songs for months, and in the studio, they record the music first. In fact, each instrument is recorded separately in the multi-track recording fashion of our time. Claire plays her guitar for this song, then the bass player, followed by the backup guitar; she starts to sing her original song called *I Knew You When*. It's an homage to her family, a tender song about sacrifices her parents made for her and how she can never pay them back.

"There are so many things I owe you for / you taught and protected me / I can never repay what you've given me / When I needed help, you held my hand. / I'm so lucky to have you in my life."

The second track is a lively song about love called *Desire*. Some of the lyrics are, "You're my favorite drink / my favorite song / We see eye to eye / I knew you before you were born / You're familiar as the back of my hand / My dreams include you."

She sings the haunting chorus of the final track of the day. "You don't see my VFW hat or my rags / but you notice my hand out / I can't live in the park or my tent for I'm always rousted / I walk down the street and you look right through me. Sometimes, you cross the street to avoid me. I drove tanks in the Gulf War / I came back broken and can't get a job anywhere." On the chorus, her backup singers sing, "I need a job and place to stay," while Claire harmonizes, "You look right through me, you look away."

On a break, Claire calls Mitch from a nearby crowded cafeteria-style Chinese restaurant to tell him the session is going well. When the call ends, a bearded man asks if he can sit at her table since there are no other empty ones. She agrees, then looks up and says, "Have I seen you before?"

"Thank you. I don't think I've seen you before."

She frowns. "I have. You were at the job site of our new house. You said you were a building inspector. You had a dizzy spell and then ran away. You had only a bushy mustache a few weeks ago. I recognize your voice."

"I'm sorry, perhaps you saw my little brother. He looks a lot like me and has a mustache. I've worn a full beard for more than a decade now. He works as a home builder in the metro area while I am lucky enough to have retired early." He puffs out his chest a bit. "I'm kind of a world traveler now." He smiles and turns on the charm. "It's nice to meet you. My name's Ash. What do you do for a living?"

"I'm engaged."

He appears crestfallen and congratulates her in a slightly hollow voice.

Claire wipes her mouth on a cloth napkin and gets up.

"Please, don't leave on my account. I'm just making conversation. Finish your lunch."

She studies his face as if to memorize it for a later time. She picks up her tray. "I lost my appetite. What's your name?"

He doesn't answer her question. "I'm sorry if I upset you. It was not my intent. The place is crowded, and I thought we could share the table and get to know each other. Share a few pleasant words while we eat. I didn't think that was such a big deal."

Her instincts tell her to leave, but then she says, "You *were* at the job site. Why are you following me?"

He huffs and puffs while his eyes dart about the grungy eating area that has rows of similar, red-checked tablecloths while faint Oriental music plays softly in the background. The average-looking bearded man appears taken aback. "Claire, you are mistaken—"

"There! How do you know my name? I didn't tell it to you!"

His grin lingers on her face, and it scares her to her bones. It feels like he's leering.

"Well, I assume that's your name from the bag on the chair next to you that is clearly marked 'Claire.'"

She laughs a bit awkwardly. "Of course. I must be going."

"Have a nice day, Claire."

She discards her uneaten food and places her plastic tray with the others on top of the trash bin before she briskly walks out. Once she rounds the corner and is out of sight, Ash reaches over for her napkin and rubs it across his face. He closes his eyes and sniffs. He stashes it in his back pocket and eats the rest of his cashew chicken while kitchen staff call out the next orders to be made.

The traditional Oriental Muzak is replaced by Claire's singing and he closes his eyes. He believes she's singing about him when he hears the lyrics to *Desire*.

After she finishes the tracks for the day, Claire returns home and packs a bag. She plans to spend the night at Mitch's after dinner on The Hill, an Italian section of St. Louis known for its good restaurants. They walk under the green awning and are on time for their reservation. The place is packed and on the noisy side tonight.

They update each other on their days, and Claire says, "I had a quick lunch at a Chinese place downtown. The place was packed, and the tables filled. You won't believe this. A guy asks to sit at my table, and I look up, and I swear it's the man from the job site, the man with the mustache who claimed he was a building inspector. The only thing was this guy had a full beard. He said he has a brother who looks like him and only has a mustache. I recognized the voice. It was the same guy. Why would he lie to me?"

"Do you think he's a stalker?"

"It's a big coincidence. The lot and then downtown at Muddy Rivers?"

"You didn't happen to take a picture of him with your phone?"

"I wish I'd thought of that when he left. It was a bit creepy."

"You see him again, call me and take a picture."

They eat their seafood ravioli and saltimbocca and return to Mitch's townhouse, where they watch a movie before making love.

Ten miles away, Ash is in bed with the pilfered napkin from the Chinese restaurant covering his face. At first, he hears singing, a song like the angels would sing in heaven. It's Claire's voice, singing sultry, sweet words directly to him, professing her love for him. The lyrics from her song *Desire* fill his ears, the exact words he longs to hear from her. Then his lips touch the faint residue of Claire's lip balm on the black cloth and he sees Mitch's bedroom, where he spies on them asleep. The blues and greens over the bed have faded to light colors, given their somnolent states. The sheet covers their intertwined legs as Claire sleeps facing Mitch, a hand on his chest. He stares at her and pleasures himself for five minutes until he summons enough mental strength to send a breath of wind into their bed that causes Claire to roll away from Mitch, revealing her naked torso to Ash. He decides she is magnificent in every way and must have her. He wishes he'd learned the arcane power to be able to transport himself to any place like his elder Roma relatives in the family album are able to do. He can't control when he can do it and when he can't. He envisions entering the bedroom and killing his therapist before he climbs into bed with his new love. She's healthy and unscarred by human tragedy and failings. She may resist him at first, but he's certain he can supersede Mitch's place in her heart. His orgasm is perhaps the most explosive he's ever had, and waves of pleasure wash over him until his breathing returns to normal. In his relaxed post-ejaculatory state, he sees them dine at Zia's earlier and longs to take Mitch's place.

He goes to bed and falls asleep. In his dream, he sees himself not in the daguerreotype picture but relaxing in his recliner in his underwear. There's a muted football game on the television, which is odd because it's summer baseball season. The clink of pots and pans and the murmur of soft voices cause his head to turn toward the little kitchen.

"Who's in the kitchen?" Then, in a brain fog and hoping beyond hope, he calls out, "Is that you, Claire?"

The clinking of pots stops, and silence fills the small house.

Sounds of shuffling feet make their way to his living room. Intoxicating cooking smells and spices waft his way.

Two old women enter his living room. He immediately recognizes the relatives from his family album. He draws a sharp intake of air but cannot get out of the recliner to run. Ropes tied around his chest and waist prevent him from rising. Bunches of purple glazer garlic tied together dangle from his neck, and the pungent smell is all over him. Both women carry knives and look so old it's difficult to guess their ages. Both short and squat women have hooked beaks for noses, wear multiple layers of colorful clothes, and appear rather overweight but move swiftly and with a bizarre grace. The same earthy smells from the woods near their village fill the living room.

"What you think, Huga?"

Ash struggles against the ropes but can't get up.

The sister pinches his cheek and pokes his belly. She removes several fresh sprigs of rosemary from his head. "I think our little Baba is ready."

Her gnarled hands and touch feel disturbingly real, and she reeks of the land. "You're not real. You can't come out of a picture from 150 years ago!"

Both ignore his words but keep smiling.

The first woman grins and raises a butcher knife. As the blade slashes toward his neck, he wakes in a sweat in his own bed.

When he walks to the kitchen that morning, there's a pot of spicy mirepoix on the stove. In with the vegetables in the unfamiliar rustic pot are rosemary sprigs, chopped purple glaze garlic, sweet paprika, and an intoxicating medley of other spices. He'd never sleepwalked to the kitchen before, and he'd never seen the iron pot before in his waking life.

He is certain he's losing his mind, for if not, the reality that this is happening is far worse.

To Phrog or Not to Phrog

He researches the concept on the internet at length before he considers it. For it to have any chance to work, he must act before security cameras are installed. Like a time-shared property, a rental, or a house with a mother-in-law quarters, a new house under construction is a perfect candidate. There's no evidence of a gun safe, and it appears neither owns any handguns. Neither owns a dog, although he's overheard them talk about getting a puppy once they're married, which would also make the idea impossible to pull off. He would need the ability to come and go at any time for this to work. He feels a rush over the voyeuristic possibilities if he can somehow pull this off. He reads stories of successful people who do this solely for a free place to stay, often for short times. They are not thieves. Most do it for food and shelter, making sure they don't eat too much food to make the owner suspicious. Some do this to obtain computer access for porn. To his way of thinking, those reasons seem picayune. He plans to do this for love.

As fall descends in St. Louis, Mitch and Claire's new home nears completion. Workers have installed the cabinets, the plumbing is in, the walls are painted, and the floors are newly installed, stained, and primed. Work is set to begin on the landscaping along with the exterior fixtures and security system. He studies the blueprints and layout of the house to scout possible hiding places and determines the small attic holds the most promise as the rafters in the garage are open. There are no acceptable hiding places in the unfinished basement. In extreme weather conditions, the attic will be hot or cold, but he doesn't anticipate being a phrogger for long.

He walks into a local hardware store to have a duplicate set of stolen keys made. It took three weeks to find the opportunity to lift the key. The one key unlocks every entry door. He also buys a sleeping bag and some portable camping gear at a sporting goods store. The next night, he enters the house with his key, climbs to the recently completed second story, and organizes the camping gear in the attic. A few stacks of extra building material are piled in the attic. He has a flashlight and a cooler. It's good to have a surprise backup plan that could be the plan given the right scenario.

He stays there for three nights, but neither Mitch nor Claire visits in the evenings. He leaves shortly before the building crew arrives each morning. He wears a sweater as the temperatures finally start to fall at night. He had a plan if Mitch were to visit alone. On the fourth night, he hears a key turn in the front door, and he hurries back to the attic. He hears Mitch and Claire talking, and they seem to be alone. They assess the lighting in each room and walk the stairs to the second floor. He holds his breath, hoping they don't bother looking in the attic. Why would they? For everyone's sake, they don't, and he loosens his grip on the gun. They return to the first floor and linger in Claire's new studio. He silently descends the attic and listens as their voices lower. A few minutes later, he realizes what is happening. It sounds as if Mitch and Claire are having sex in her new studio. He carefully climbs down to the first floor without making a sound and peers around a corner. Claire is lying on a table, her ass hanging off the side, and Mitch is standing between her legs with his pants around his ankles, pumping away while their noises and grunts intensify. Their auras of brilliant blues and greens spin and dance above them until the colors explode and turn white for a moment before the colors return and slow. He wanted to dash the back of Mitch's head in with a crowbar, but that would hardly be the way to win Claire's love.

He stealthily walks to the second-floor steps and stands there while the two lovers laugh and giggle. He hears them readjust their clothing.

"My, my. That was quite a christening of my music room!"

"I'm glad you didn't want to wait, either. That was intense!"

"Good idea you thought to relock the door after we came in. Just to be sure, no one walked in on us."

He smirks and says to himself: *If you only knew.*

He hears Claire enter a bathroom and use the toilet.

Mitch runs a hand along the fireplace mantle. "Shall we stop at Manno's for a dirty martini?"

"Works for me, hon."

He climbs the stairs as the couple makes their way toward the marble front landing. His foot accidentally kicks the attic door.

"Did you hear that?" Claire says.

"No. Probably the house settling is all."

"Let's see the view at night from the second-floor patio before we go," Claire suggests.

He slowly walks into the attic and shuts the door behind him, just in case. He listens as their footfalls come ever closer to his hiding place.

Three feet away, with only the door between them, Claire says, "If we want to store out-of-season clothes somewhere, the attic will do just fine."

She raps her knuckles on the attic door while Ash grips the handle of his gun tighter.

He holds his breath and holds the knob in case she decides to open the door.

Instead, he hears the sliding glass door whoosh open, and the two step out onto the second-floor balcony. "Look at the nighttime view!" Claire says.

Mitch agrees. "This will be a great place to read, overlooking the lake and woods. You can write lyrics here, too. It's very peaceful."

"My dad is already talking about fishing in the lake. The contractor said five-pound bass and eight-pound catfish have already been caught by residents."

Mitch grunts as he pulls the sliding door closed. "I need to tell Derek this slider is sticking. Should be an easy fix."

He waits until they leave and does not follow. He leaves his supplies in the attic and goes home. He decides to drink alcohol and take sleeping pills to lessen any chance of dreaming, and tonight, it works. He wakes up at noon feeling groggy and depressed. He doesn't know what to do about the relatives and the family album. Would destroying the album do any good, or would doing so trap the old women in this world? He places multiple calls to his remaining contacts in Hungary and describes his situation to them. They all say he's mistaken, that not even Romanis can come out of pictures, and one ventures so far as to tell him he's crazy. The true *gypsies* he met with when he was in Roma don't have phones or refuse to come to the phone. He imagines them laughing and smiling at his plight.

He calls Mitch's office and makes his usual end-of-the-day Friday appointment.

The Final Appointment

Ash places items in a briefcase before he showers and dresses for his appointment. He may or may not need these things, depending on how the situation unfolds. His living room carries the faint odor of the land and mulch from the woods in the old country, or at least he thinks it still does, and he can smell the pot of vegetables and spices in the kitchen even though he threw out the pot and all yesterday. He suspects his ability to discriminate reality from fantasy may be impaired.

He considers another possible explanation for these bizarre happenings that, somehow, he's being haunted by one of these old family members who must have died more than a century and a half ago, but that doesn't do him much good. What can you do to respond to a haunting?

He sits with his briefcase in the waiting room until Mitch invites him inside. He looks at the clock that gives the time as 4:35. He's running a bit late today.

Mitch sits down. "Did you introduce yourself to the woman you're attracted to, like I suggested?"

He smirks that the session starts with this question. "I did, in a rather round-about way, but I don't think she's interested. I think I came on too strong."

"How did you come on too strong, in a round-about way?"

"I don't think she liked my presentation because before I could introduce myself, she shot me down and said she was engaged. My timing may have been bad."

"Well, she's also engaged. As the old saying goes, there's a lot of other fish in the sea."

"I tried to tell myself that, but there's something incredibly special about this woman. And engaged means not yet married."

"How do you know she has special qualities if you didn't talk with her and get to know her?"

He can't get into that without revealing one of his superpowers. "Just from observing her, I got the sense there was much more than meets the eye. She is a beauty who comports herself with dignity, grace, and kindness. There's a quiet confidence in her. I found myself drawn to her, wanting to be around her. I still do. If it's meant to be, it's meant to be."

Mitch makes a mental note that he didn't say, 'if it's *not* meant to be.'

Noticing his unkempt hair and budding bags under his eyes, Mitch says, "Are you sleeping okay? You look tired today."

His eyebrows raise. He glances above Mitch's head and sees blues and greens spinning a bit faster. "Is it that obvious? I've been sleeping like crap and having nightmares to the point where I find myself wanting to stay awake. Lately, I've been taking a sleeping pill with alcohol to knock myself out. Maybe it's all catching up to me."

"Alcohol and pills are not a good combination, as you likely know. Is there a recurring theme to these nightmares?"

He pauses and lowers his voice. "I don't know if I should tell you. They're bone-jarringly scary, and if I share them, you're going to think I'm psychotic and losing my mind. Nothing like this has ever happened to me, and if I share this with you, I cannot unshare it."

"That sounds rather ominous. I'm not certain I could call you psychotic based on your dreams."

He exhales a big breath and closes his eyes. "I must share this with you, for everyone's sake. You remember I told you I visited my country of origin several times."

Mitch nods and waits for him to continue. "I must provide you some context before I speak of these dreams." Ash describes the burgs in Hungary, where he traced his Roma roots. Then he mentions the family album. He removes it from the briefcase but doesn't open it. He fiddles anxiously with the many different colored strings that hang from it.

"I compiled this album from numerous sources, many from town elders that people in this country would describe as shady at best. In other words, people in early years Americans would call gypsies. The first written accounts of my ancestors said gypsies were called the descendants of Cain in the 14th century. Over the next four centuries, the gypsies, who started out in northern India a thousand years earlier, crossed every kingdom and principality in Europe. They drove and operated out of multi-colored horse-drawn caravans from which they sold their goods and plied their trades, or they lived in small, oblong black tents or sometimes in caves. They wore brightly colored clothing, with many layers and sashes and bandanas. They told fortunes and sold trinkets and other wares. It was written by other people that wherever they lived, gypsies didn't stay long because that place would soon become full of vermin and filth. By the 18th century, they traveled to America, and today, they live all over the world. Some of my relatives in the old country still live in the traditional manner, migrating and avoiding major cities, but most gypsies have assimilated into the larger societies around them."

"You're describing the Roma or Romani people."

He nods. "At least most people now consider the word 'gypsies,' to be politically correct and downright insulting. As I alluded to, many have married into the local populations yet still manage to retain their distinct identity. These leaders held much knowledge about fortune-telling and herbal remedies that were passed down orally for many generations to the next. Their way of life is steeped in mystery and mysticism. My ancestors used tarot cards, crystal balls, and read palms. Their knowledge can reveal important insights into the past, present, and future. Their superstitions can bring good luck, ward off bad luck, or cause bad luck. Family is an essential part of the culture, and they believe in the power of nature, and many of their traditions revolve around fire, water, and earth."

He pauses.

"Do you believe these old relatives possessed powers in real life?"

He gulps. "After my visits to the old country, I do."

"Is that the context? Tell me about your dreams."

"One more thing. When I visited Hungary on three separate occasions, every elder sensed the lengthy history of deaths in my history. I didn't share it with them, but they divined it with their fortune-telling and asked me about it. Since family is paramount in the culture, I sensed I was being ostracized." He places his hand on the cover and taps it. "During the third visit, I was asked to leave once I compiled this family album."

"Do you consider yourself a part of their culture?"

"I don't know. I used to think not, but it is where my family came from. My DNA came from Hungary, and then there's this damn picture."

Mitch finds it interesting he doesn't think he's fully assimilated into the American culture. "Go on."

Ash runs a palm over the heavy album. "I brought the album today as proof. There is an old daguerreotype photo in here that dates to the early 1840s. The two wrinkled elderly women in it were distant relatives long dead. They're posing in front of a fire in a rural village with a pot of stew cooking on an open flame." He takes a deep breath and exhales. "All but one of the last times I looked at it, they were not in the picture."

"Can we look at the picture together?"

He slowly nods his head again. "It's on the third page." Ash tenses noticeably before he hands the heavy album to him. "You look at it."

Mitch places it in his lap and examines the cover. "This looks very old. Where did you find the album?"

"Toward the rear of a brightly colored gypsy caravan in the rural section of a little burg. The old man said some of the strings contained gold and other precious metals, but when I had it appraised back in the States, the professionals said it didn't. Still, I got a good price for it, and it is a one-of-a-kind piece."

Mitch opens the cover and looks at the old letters on the first page. "Do you mind if I read the translations on the right?" He hopes they may lend insight into his new client.

"Go ahead."

There is a picture above the letter written in Romani. "Is that your father and mother?"

"Yes. He worked as a butcher in the States after he and my mother immigrated from Hungary and entered New York Harbor. Mom was a housewife. We lived in New York and gradually came west over the decades."

Mitch smiles. "That's a touching letter. Clearly, he wanted you to have the promise of a new and better life. You bear a striking resemblance to your father." He reads the letter from his mother. "She intimates your parents sacrificed everything for you. You were certainly loved, am I right?"

"I was. I never had pictures or knowledge of my grandparents or their parents since everyone in my family died so young." He sits back in the chair. "The next picture is the one in question. They were called maternal aunts, Anna and Stella, the only people in my family to make it to old age."

Mitch turns the page and looks at the picture in question. He quickly thumbs through the rest of the pages and returns to the one in question. His face is impassive when he turns the book toward Ash. "These two women standing next to the fireplace, right?"

Ash holds his breath and sees the women exactly where they should be. No movement, no hair out of place. No smoke rising. The picture is back to normal. Stella is the one who flew in the air and caught him in the forest in his dream, while Anna told her sister her little Baba was ripe for the cookpot. He doesn't know what to make of this and has no words.

"There are no other pictures of the scene in the album. Are these the women you say left the picture?"

He frowns. His voice sounds hollow, confused. "Yes, they are. They were gone!" He's amazed they've returned to the photo.

"What if you're mistaken? Did something frighten you earlier that day? Did you see these women in your home? If so, were they threatening?"

He shifts in his chair. "I was alone at home when it happened. I told you I'd had some wine at dinner and settled into my chair with a beer to look at the album. When I first looked at it, both women had appeared to shift position and glared at me, and I swear their eyes followed mine. I threw the book down and wondered if I were losing my mind."

"What did you do next?"

Ash stares at him without answering. "I panicked. I got up and made sure all the doors and windows were locked, and I brought out the gun from my nightstand. I searched the closets and rooms, then finally went to bed cradling the gun."

"Did you ever see them in your house or anywhere else?"

Ash answers yes, then starts to say no, then says, "I'm not sure."

"What do you mean?"

"I may have been dreaming the times it happened." He describes in detail the dreams he had when he woke up with leaves and dirt in his pajamas, and the one of being tied to his chair, and the strange pot in his kitchen simmering the aromatic mirepoix. "I felt their hands on me. I have never sleepwalked. Honestly, I don't know if I was in a dream state or not."

"Is that true? You're not certain you weren't transported to rural Hungary from your bed that night and that during another night in bed, you were somehow tied to your recliner when you lived alone?"

He hesitates a long time before answering. "No, I don't know for sure."

Mitch briefly looks at his phone after it beeps. Claire texted him that she was in the outer office, and he realized they'd run fifteen minutes late. "Do you feel unsafe in your home?"

Another pause. "No, but I don't feel good about two old women trying to kill me and put me in a stewpot."

Mitch realizes the juxtaposition of his next question. "Do you believe someone is trying to harm you?"

He shakes his head in frustration. "Honestly, it makes no sense, but maybe. If not, then I've been cursed by someone from the old country."

"If this is indeed a gypsy curse, why were you asked to leave Romani?"

He struggles to find an answer. "Perhaps because of all the deaths in my family?"

Mitch exhales. "We've run over. Let's meet again at four next Friday. Write down any dreams or events that happen between now and then. Call my pager if you think you need to. I think this is in your mind. You believe 'gypsies' possess certain supernatural powers, and that, coupled with stress, has caused these misinterpretations of reality."

Ash grabs his briefcase and exits via the privacy door, and several seconds later, Claire screams.

Mitch rushes into the hallway to see Claire pointing at his client. "That's him! This is the man who wore a mustache when he posed as a building inspector and later wore a beard when he stalked me at the Chinese restaurant downtown."

Mitch turns to his client. "Is this true?"

Ash shrugs and sees the black aura spinning over Claire's head. He could hardly deny it when she came out of the women's room and saw him heading for the men's room. "It is."

"Why?" Claire asks.

He turns to her with an air of confidence, thinking honesty remains the best policy. "I'm in love with you. We should be together, not you and him."

Amazed, she crosses her arms and huffs. "You don't even know me."

"I know more about you than you think."

"I am in love with Mitch. He and I will be married. You need to accept that and move on with your life."

Graduate school doesn't prepare you for something this bizarre, Mitch thinks to himself. "Ash, let's go back to the office and continue our talk for a moment." He waits until Ash walks back into his office before, he whispers the words *go to where we met on our first date* to Claire.

Once seated, Mitch says, "So, Claire is the woman you were interested in that I suggested you meet and talk to after our last session?"

He nods affirmatively.

"Did you know she's in a relationship with me prior to this?"

"I did."

"How?"

He chooses to lead with honesty. His voice rises in pitch and sounds hollow like he's replaying events in his mind. "After our initial session, I lingered outside the front of the Sevens Building and saw you leave. On a whim, I decided to follow you as you walked to a restaurant, where you met Claire for dinner. I fell in love with her when I watched you two interact. I followed you two several times. I attended both her concerts and was the other one who sent her flowers. I know you two had sex in her new studio when you visited the house a few nights ago."

Mitch feels his blood pressure rise higher, and his breathing is shallow. "Why do you say that?"

His smile becomes a smirk, his voice more forceful than ever. "I could have killed you several times during any of the occasions I followed you."

His brow furrows briefly, and he ignores the last remark. "I'm confused. The man who told me he thinks he should be alone for the rest of his life because the women he meets have all died suddenly decides to attach himself to a woman without knowing anything about her?"

Ash decides to continue with brutal honesty. "I know this may scare you. Claire has an adorable beauty mark shaped like Italy high on the outside of her right thigh that is not visible when she wears a skirt."

Mitch feels his breathing grow more shallow. Every word Ash has said made his skin crawl. "How do you think you know that?"

He tries not to smile but can't avoid it. "I know it's true. I have not shared everything about me with you but now is the time. I have abilities precious few people in this country possess. Abilities that I assume must have been unwittingly handed down to me from my parents, for they never taught them to me." He tells Mitch how he won six different lotteries; he describes his ability to see colors like thought bubbles above the heads of people when they talk, which provides him information about their relationship; and he says when he dreams, he can enter the lives of people past or present if he's touched them or if he's seen them on TV or if he has an item they've come in contact with that day. "I've relived more atrocities and crimes in my sleep than you've read about."

He doesn't mention his ability to know Claire's dearth of history of loss or her rosy physical health.

Mitch can't resist asking, "How do you think you know of her beauty mark?"

Ash tells him about the napkin from the Chinese restaurant and seeing her in Mitch's bed that night in his mind's eye after he describes Mitch's bedroom in specific and chilling detail.

Mitch's stomach does a barrel roll. He briefly entertains the highly unlikely possibility that somehow Ash broke into his townhouse, circumvented his alarm system, and installed hidden cameras but rules it out. *Does my patient want to kill and replace me?* "I don't believe you. That's impossible."

"I have these powers, and that's why I know the elderly women from my family album have been in my house."

He thinks: *is there a way to use his beliefs against him*? "No, they have not."

The smirk remains. "We are at an impasse."

"No, we're not. Why do you think Claire and I had sex in the new house we're building?"

He continues to lead with honesty and hands Mitch a key. "I watched you. I was inside when you two visited that night. I have a cozy little set-up in the attic. Feel free to check it yourself at your leisure. I left a green sleeping bag, an orange ice cooler, and other sundries, but I no longer need to hide there. It was touch-and-go that night when Claire almost opened the attic door when the two of you went to the second story to see the nighttime view over the lake. I believe she said the attic would be a good place to store out-of-season clothes." He looks at the key clutched in Mitch's hand. "Don't worry, it's the only key I have."

Mitch sits flabbergasted by the eerie calmness and self-control in Ash's voice. The matter-of-fact way he speaks has twisted Mitch's stomach in knots. It's as if he fully expects Mitch to step out of the way and allow him to be with Claire. Ash's words sound like an adult telling his misbehaving child how the situation will play out. Danger has once again entered Mitch's life in the form of an unbalanced client.

He makes sure to keep his voice on an even keel. "You're misinterpreting reality. You are seeing and imagining things that simply are not there. People don't come alive from an old picture. No one can envision winning lottery numbers after a sweat. Rational people don't profess undying love for a woman they do not know. You cannot transport yourself into other people's homes with your mind. Now, you're acting on these false beliefs—stalking people and more. You protect yourself with a gun from the women in the picture. You say you could have killed me. You're having a psychotic break, and there are medicines that can help. The best thing for you is to agree to a brief psychiatric stay—"

Ash shakes his head. He reaches into his briefcase and produces the gun. "I'm not going back to a damn loony bin."

Mitch stares at the black hole of the barrel and then forces himself to look Ash in the eyes. He tries his best to maintain an outward calm. "Back? You said you had no psychiatric history. What else have you not told me?"

The smirk leaves his face, and a strange blackness overcomes it. "It doesn't matter anymore."

They stare at each other for a minute until Ash stands. "I'm going to find my love. Don't interfere, and I will let you live."

He backs out of the office and runs to the elevators.

Mitch exhales and calls the lobby downstairs to describe Ash to building security and tells them to call the police. He calls Claire and updates her on Ash, suggesting she stay at the place where they met on their first date and stay there until she hears from him. Next, he completes and signs the necessary paperwork to involuntarily commit Ash to a 96-hour hold in a psychiatric facility, legal in the state of Missouri, given his mental state and current propensity for harm. The forms are notarized so the county police can pick Ash up and accompany him to a facility.

Security called back an hour later to report they didn't detain or even see Ash exit the building. Mitch contacted the county police and faxed the commitment papers to their office so their officers could serve him the papers. He warns them Ash may be armed with at least a handgun.

Before he leaves the office for the day, Mitch creates a list of area therapists for Ash that do not see clients in the Sevens Building to consider seeing since Ash has overstepped the boundaries of the client/therapist relationship and threatened Mitch and Claire. He sends a certified copy of the letter to the address Ash provided. He calls Ash on his cell and leaves a message that he can no longer be his therapist and to expect a list of potential replacement therapists in the mail. His last act that day is to meet with security and they find his picture on CCTV. They are instructed that if Ash enters the Sevens Building in the future, they are to detain him and contact the police. He says he may be armed and could wear a disguise such as a fake mustache or beard.

Mitch calls Claire on her cell, and she asks if he's okay.

"I'm fine. Are you? You still at the statue?"

She says she is.

"Great. I'm walking to my car and will meet you there soon."

He meets her at the statue of Stan Musial near gate four at Busch Memorial Stadium, and they walk to Ballpark Village. They order drinks and whiskey onion rings to share. He updates her on the rest of his interactions with Ash and the precautions he's taken.

"He sounds like he's really sick."

Mitch takes a sip and nods.

"Do you think we're in danger?"

Mitch thanks the waitress when the rings arrive. "Probably not, but I don't want to take any chances in the immediate future. I think we should stay together for a couple of days, whether it's your place or mine. My hope is the police find him at home and escort him to the nearest psych facility to get him on anti-psychotics and get him stabilized. If that happens, the facility will contact me before he's discharged."

They stop at her Clayton apartment, and she packs a bag to stay with Mitch in his townhouse for the weekend.

The Fight of His Life

Ash returns home and packs his own bag. He stays at a hotel not far from his home in case Mitch sends the cops to his door to take him against his will to a mental ward. Before he goes, he tosses the family album inside a suitcase, locks it, and throws it in the back of a closet. He returns each day for his mail, and he watches his house in case the police come looking for him. Two uniformed officers knock on his door twice the first week and call his phone that he doesn't answer.

He rips up the certified letter from Mitch.

He visits their new home to find the second key he had made no longer opens the doors so he throws it away.

Two weeks later, he checks out of the hotel and returns home after he meets at length with his lawyer and financial planner. The comfort that his affairs are in order feels infinitesimal and superfluous, but at least he knows they're in place for the time being. He can always amend them if his situation changes down the road. The meetings also remind him that his accounts have dwindled over the years, so he makes plans before the last week of this year's Indian summer.

He packs his car and drives to an isolated farm area in rural Washington County near Potosi, where his last sweat took place. He bought the isolated, five-acre wooded farmland ten years ago, and the only man-made structures on the property are a battered single-wide mobile home and a rusty old aluminum shed. He stores the few supplies he brought into the mobile home after he noticed that someone had broken into the home and squatted since he was last here. The inside has a smell of ammonia or urine, and the large number of empty Sudafed boxes and two-liter bottles outside on the ground indicates the home had been used to cook meth. He opens the windows and doors to air out the trailer.

In two days, the temperature will top out at 89, and he needs to clear the area for his sweat. Due to his fear of snakes, he uses a scythe instead of the old brush hog in the shed to remove the growth of brush, saplings, and weeds since his last visit. While he does this in a clearing where there is no shade, he drinks and eats as little as possible to prepare for his sweat. Once the brush is cleared, he finds the wooden door in the ground, and it opens with a reluctant groan. He cleans the small, low space of leaves, sticks, and old charcoal before he checks to make sure the ventilation system has remained clear. He piles wood at the far end of the space and places a blanket by the door where he will lay.

He sleeps in his car both nights due to the stench inside the trailer. He misses Claire, so he covers his face with the cloth napkin from the Chinese store, but he only receives some vague, dreamlike images of her. He wakes up tired and achy after a dreamless and restless sleep.

When the temperature hits 80, he strips naked and lays on a blanket in the clearing for hours without food or water. He closes his eyes and listens to the sounds of the woods. Birds chatter and bugs land on him while later, a brace of pheasants and a lone white-tailed deer amble near the small clearing. When the temperature peaks at 90, he walks to the sweat, climbs in, and closes the door. He starts the fire and sits cross-legged on the blanket, a small flashlight next to him. Sparks from the fire land on him, and he brushes them off. He keeps one eye on the fire and the other on the ventilation system. The heat becomes intense, and his eyes water and turn red from the copious smoke, but the ventilation system appears to be working. Several times, he considers leaving for his own safety, but he resists the urge. At some point, he passes out and sees himself in a dank basement as large as a cavern. Two figures sit before him, tied to chairs. Stella and Anna look up at him with abject fear in their eyes. Between their chairs, a stoked fire blazes, and in it, a branding iron glows red-hot. He grabs the handle and raises it to Stella's forehead. Before he brands her, he wakes up to find his own head is inches from the fire. He's disoriented from the smoke, and there's a burning pain in his leg. He looks down and sees the fire consuming the blanket as it spreads toward him. He raises up and throws the blanket over the fire, which doubles the smoke in the tiny room. He fumbles blindly for the tiny flashlight and locates the door handle, for if he doesn't get out of the sweat now, he will die in this tiny hole in the ground. With what ebbing strength that remains, he throws his weight against the door until it budges and finally creaks open. Coughing, he lies in the now-dark clearing and rolls on his back to see the clearest sky he's ever seen in Missouri. Ursa Minor, Ursa Major, and Draco are all visible in his tear-filled eyes. While he looks to the sky, coughing smoke from his lungs, the stars realign themselves into six numbers, and when he blinks, they're back in their rightful place in the night sky. The way in which the numbers reveal themselves during a sweat has always been unique; this middle-of-the-night divulgence is no exception.

He hobbles to the trailer to drink and throw water on his face. He writes down what he hopes are the numbers before he showers, thankful he paid the utility bills here for the last ten years.

It's three in the morning, and today is the next lottery drawing. He has until seven PM to get his tickets. He never knows which lottery the numbers belong to, so he buys a ticket with the same numbers for each different, six-number lottery. He spends hours rehydrating and cooling down before he can entertain the notion of safely driving home. At dawn, he douses the wood in the sweat with water to make sure there can be no more chance of fire in the woods.

The following day, he hits the Powerball lottery with five of the six numbers. He guessed the wrong number for the red Powerball out of the six numbers, but he still wins two million dollars.

He rests for the week to restore his strength until he decides to follow Claire the next Saturday.

After showering, he walks into his bedroom and chooses his clothes for the day. When he turns toward the bed, he freezes. The suitcase sits on it, and a long slash mark has cut the outer fabric. He inches closer to find the album is gone. He dresses in a hurry and opens the nightstand drawer where his gun should be but finds it empty.

He reaches a decision: *When I find that accursed album, I'm burning it.*

He searches the small house and cannot find it. Having time to kill before he drives to Claire's apartment, he turns the television on to a cooking show. He's seen the female British host before but can't recall her name. Barefoot, she almost always has a glass of wine in one hand and her voice has a bored quality to it, which to him should fly in the face of audience interest. He walks to the kitchen for a cup of black coffee.

Static fills the television screen until it shows the host talking from her studio kitchen about today's recipe when the doorbell rings. Ash puts the steaming cup on his TV tray, looks through the peephole, and opens the front door to find no one is there. He changes the channel when he learns today's dish is goulash.

Later, he drives to Claire's apartment and rings the bell, but there is no answer. A swing by their new house and Mitch's townhouse doesn't find her hybrid car, either. He parks back at her Clayton apartment and reads a book for the rest of the afternoon. He rings her bell, with no answer again, so he leaves a gift. A concoction of red wine, dried and crushed basil leaves, dried fennel, dried European Vervain flowers, and ground nutmeg. The night before, Ash boiled the potion for three minutes, let it cool, and strained it through cheesecloth, then sweetened it with honey. He drinks half of it just now in the car and the rest he leaves at Claire's front door with a note saying, 'Thinking of you, I think you will love this brew. Enjoy it now while fresh! M.'

Maybe he should have staked out Mitch's townhouse instead and decided to do so on Sunday. Stakeouts take their toll on your body when you sit in a car all day.

At 10:30 PM, he goes for a jog through Shaw Park in Clayton. Most people are exiting since the park closes at eleven, but Ash stretches and runs the wide paths as a few straggling dog walkers head for the exits to their parked cars and large and small groups of picnickers pack up their belongings and trudge from the park pavilions. It's a park he's never been in, but it's close to Claire's place and he knows she's jogged there. As he continues to run, he notices fewer people around him in the lighted pathways in the dark.

Rounding a bend, he sees her! Dressed in an all-white tracksuit, Claire appears like a vision out of the darkness a hundred yards ahead; a white headband keeps the sweat from her face and eyes. He revels in the fluid action when her hips sway as she runs and notices her suit seems to twinkle every now and then when they pass an overhead light. She quickens her pace for twenty minutes, which makes him do the same until they are across from a barbecue pit. Growing fatigued, he admires her backside while he speeds up a final time and, from ten yards behind, calls her name. His body tenses. He's waited so long for this moment and hopes she drank the wine. She stops, so he does the same. She turns around, and the dawn of recognition fills her face. There is no fear, no panic in her look. Instead, the smile on her face is ear-to-ear. They stride closer to each other, and her smile widens. Her eyes seem to glow. He's so happy he's near tears. It's going exactly as he hoped.

"Did you drink the wine I left for you, Claire?"

Up close, something seems slightly off about her. When she speaks, it takes too long for the sound to leave her throat, and when it does, her voice sounds as if it's coming from somewhere else, somehow.

"I did. It made me feel warm and happy. Heat and contentment filled my body. I guess I have you to thank for that?"

He takes a final step so close to her he can lean forward and kiss her. He sees himself reflected in her eyes and in that instant, he knew everything in his life with her was going to work out. "Yes! That was exactly what was supposed to happen. I love you, Claire, and now I know you love me. You and I should move into that new house together. Mitch will find someone else. He always does."

She, again, is a beat or two too slow to respond. He thinks his eyes must be deceiving him when he swears he can see right through her when she moves even closer. She whispers into his ear, "Do you have another bottle of that gypsy love potion, Ash?"

Fully aroused, he leans forward to kiss her when he realizes what's wrong. He freezes at her final words. "How ... how did you know I'd be here?

Instead of kissing Claire's full, pouting lips, her face morphs into the haggard one of Stella. He kisses the thin lips of the old crow that smells of woodland mildew a moment before the old woman slits his throat. "It is your time, Baba." In an instant, Anna flies in from over the treetops and helps her sister carry him to a nearby barbecue pit, where they hang him upside down so his blood continues to stain the ground red.

Ash tries to speak, but the best sounds he can make are weak gurgling ones. Panic fills his face. His extremities flail until his lungs fill with blood and the last of his precious air leaves his body. The last thing he sees before blood drips into his eyes is an upside-down view of a bubbling cauldron on a roaring fireplace like the one he threw out from his kitchen weeks ago. The aroma is the same enticing, complex one as the one from his nightmare.

Anna steps forward and slices his cheeks off while Ash is still alive. The last words he hears are the terse dialogue of the sisters.

"We must hurry, Stella. The park staff will make a final sweep of the grounds."

He feels excruciating pain like a colony of angry bees has landed on his face, as Anna throws his cheeks into the pot.

"Next, take Baba's ribs and belly meat. That will make the stew perfect."

"You're right, sister." When Anna carefully cuts into Ash's midsection to avoid his internal organs, she cracks his ribs and removes them. His heart finally stops, along with his agony.

The sisters fly off with the cauldron of hot stew between them, and half an hour later, park staff find a most grisly and bloody spectacle.

A Move, a Declaration, and a Reading

A month later, Mitch and Claire move into their new home on a crisp fall day. Moving crews unload and set up the large furniture, including Claire's piano, while everyone else hauls boxes and small items. At the end of the moving day, they cater Italian food for their friends as a thank you. Claire's parents, Samantha and Mark Kelly had flown in from San Diego earlier that day for the move and to meet Jean and Alan Adams for the second time. Luckily, the two sets of parents seem to genuinely enjoy each other's company. After dinner, the parents and friends sit and drink and talk around the living room fireplace. Jean and Alan offer to drive the Kellys to their hotel so Mitch and Claire can settle in for their first night as their friends gradually leave.

At the end of their week off from work, Claire receives a call from a stranger.

"Miss Kelly, my name is John Fincher, an attorney with Goldman and Davies. I'm handling the estate of Mr. Ashton Farkas. I have good news for you. You stand to inherit the entirety of Mr. Farka's estate, as he died childless and with no known surviving relatives."

"Who?"

When he repeats the name, she says, "Ash? There must be some mistake. I didn't know him." She wants to add, "Nor did I want to know him," but she chooses not to.

"You are aware of his death a month ago?"

"Yes, my friend showed me the brief article in the paper."

"He certainly knew you. He has your personal information, and from the looks of his records and photographs, I assumed you two were dating."

"To be brutally honest, I did not know him at all."

Fincher clears his throat. "I don't what to say about that other than you are the sole beneficiary of his house, bank accounts, and all his property. There is a significant amount of money in his estate. If you'd like, I suggest we meet in person to discuss this." He hesitates. "Are you certain he never mentioned he was leaving everything to you at some point in your relationship?"

He was my stalker. "Trust me, I'm certain."

She makes the appointment.

Mitch accompanies her to the Clayton meeting after he pulls the brief article from the Post-Dispatch and re-reads it:

Brutal Murder in St. Louis Park

Police found partial remains of an unidentified body of a white male believed to be in his 30s or 40s late after closing two nights ago in Shaw Park. The naked body was found in a bloody area near one of the BBQ areas with his clothes near the scene. No evidence of a struggle, and the clothes seem to indicate the man may have been a jogger or walker. If anyone witnessed any unusual events that took place in the park that night, please contact the Clayton Police Department at (314) 645-3000.

The only other mention in the Post came after the remains were identified as those of Ashton Farkas, with the same plea to those who may have information about the murder to call the Clayton Police Department.

The law offices of Goldman and Davies are not flashy or staffed by many ancillary workers. The woman at the front desk offers them bottled water while they wait fifteen minutes past the meeting time.

A paunchy, balding man in an ill-fitting suit and penny loafers introduces himself as John Fincher and escorts them to a small office. He makes idle chit-chat about the weather while they walk. Sweat appears on his brow, and he appears nervous.

He hands Claire a packet of papers. "On top is a copy of Mr. Farka's notarized Last Will and Testament. As you can see, he mentions you as the sole beneficiary of the entirety of his financial holdings and all his property, which includes his home, car, and items contained inside both.

Claire frowns. "You're right, but I still don't understand why he would do this. He didn't know me."

Fincher pushes his glasses higher up on his nose. "I think I can enlighten you. He changed his will about a week before his …death. He was clearly smitten with you; dare I say, he was in love with you, as evidenced by the next page."

Claire flips the will over and reads a letter addressed to her:

My Dearest Claire:

If you're reading this letter, it means I'm dead. I had such great plans for us. I knew we were soulmates from the time I first saw you in that Clayton restaurant. Not only are you beautiful and talented, but inside, you're perfect and seemingly untouched by how hard the world is and how family and relationships wear people down over time. The greatest regret in my life is not making you my wife. You could have saved me, and I, you. You are, and will always be, the love of my life. I hope that the emptiness you must feel in your heart at my passing will lessen in time.

My life was difficult, at best. No one in my family is alive in the traditional sense, and the women I've known have all left me, via death, save for you. I've had zero luck in the girlfriend department until I saw you. I planned to woo you and build a great life together wherever you wanted to live. I knew so much about you before we ever met and I apologize if I ever hurt or scared you. I wish we'd gotten to know each other better.

Members of my family probably killed me, and I don't know why. I visited the old country on many occasions and looked forward to taking you there. Perhaps I upset the people from my homeland, but I will never know.

I'm sorry we were separated by my murder. I hope you forever keep a place in your heart for me.

I also apologize for making Dr. Adams feel uncomfortable, so please pass my regrets on to him, but tell him I was right. He will know what I'm talking about.

I leave you everything I own, and my hope is that, in some small way, it adds a level of comfort to your life without me in it. I hope to look down on you from heaven every day.

All my love,

Ashton Farkas

Fincher notices her knitted brow in response to the letter and shrugs while she passes it to Mitch, whom she'd introduced earlier as her fiancé. "I apologize for asking this, but weren't you and Ashton in love?"

She wanted to say he was a stalker, but she refrained. "No, he was … infatuated with me. I never even properly met the man."

"Huh," Fincher says. "He also requests that his remains be cremated and given to you."

The look on Claire's face is one of utter surprise.

Fincher turns to Mitch. "He mentions you in his letter …"

Mitch straightens from a slight slouch. "He does."

Time goes by in an uncomfortable silence until Mr. Fincher says, "How did you know him, and what is he referring to when he says he was right about something?"

He shakes his head. "It's safe to say I didn't know him at all, either."

Claire puts down the paper copies. "I don't want anything from him, especially his ashes."

Fincher swivels his chair back to her. "I anticipate his financial interests, minus the few remaining outstanding debts his estate must pay off, should be north of 1.9 million dollars. His house and car are conservatively estimated to be valued at 200K."

Claire immediately folds her arms over her chest. "I don't want anything from him."

"The man apparently had no one else in his circle and was murdered in a public setting. How about you go home and think about it for a few days? Can you do that? A lot of good can be done with that kind of money, whether you want to accept it or not."

She confers with Mitch and reluctantly agrees.

The next day at noon, Mitch's longtime frenemy-turned-friend Detective Baker of City Homicide calls his phone and says, "Open the door, Breezy."

Mitch and Claire let in the massive bald black man to their new home. Baker wears his traditional black outfit, complete with jeans, boots, and a leather jacket. Next to him stands a pudgy white man in a brown suit and hat with a yellow tie, his arms loaded with packages and an eighteen-pack of Heineken.

They step into the living room, and Baker whistles his approval. "Nice new digs, my man."

Claire notices the stranger burdened with packages and helps him carry them to the kitchen island. She sees thick steaks, massive shrimp, garlic bread, and salad. "Am I right to assume we're having a welcome into the new house party, JoJo?"

He hugs and kisses her. "You said the magic phrase, little lady!"

To them both, he says, "Oh, where are my damn manners? This here is my friend Detective Stone of Clayton PD. They introduce themselves and shake hands with Stone.

Mitch says, "I imagine you're here because of the murder of Ashton Farkas."

Baker smiles. "We're here to celebrate your beautiful new place (I love the modern style of the home from the outside!) and to ask Claire about her relationship with the deceased. Detective Stone requested my presence since the two of you are friends of mine, but I only agreed if we could turn this little visit into a friendly time to celebrate your new house.

Stone steps forward, and the four sit around the kitchen table. "There are several irregularities in the case, and I thought Detective Baker's presence might help." He looks to Baker, who nods.

Stone produces a folder. "These have not been released to the public, but this was the scene the park staff came upon a mere thirty minutes after the park closed that day." Claire puts her hand over her face, and Mitch grimaces as they look at a picture of the remains of the trussed-up corpse of Ash, a close-up of his abdomen minus the ribs, a close-up shot of his face where the cheeks were sliced off, and final pictures of the messy barbecue pit five feet away with the gray coals and little pockets of red fire still glowing in them.

Stone sips a glass of water before he continues while Baker twists open a Heineken. "The drops of blood near the grill matched Mr. Farka's coagulated blood beneath his body, as well as specks of blood on the grill itself. The body was moved from the jogging path to the barbecue pit, and blood was found between the spots. It's reasonable to assume the perpetrator or perps grilled parts of Mr. Farkas for the purpose of consuming him, but there was no trace of discarded bones, meat, or the suspect's blood anywhere else in the park.

"My team conducted interviews of everybody we could find in the park late that night and the only thing a couple remembered seeing was a woman jogging the paths with a man jogging behind her. It was too dark for a reliable description, but the witnesses said the lady jogger may have been you. No one recalls seeing anyone grilling at that BBQ grill beyond seven PM. I assume the perps could have quickly grilled the select parts and placed them in a container, but again, no one remembers seeing people who fit that description leaving from that section of the park near closing time. We did talk to a young couple who claimed they saw Santa and two of his reindeer that night fly over the park as they walked along Brentwood Boulevard, but they were stoners who admitted to smoking pot that night.

"None of his neighbors admit to knowing anything about Mr. Farkas. He was quiet, kept to himself, and never caused a problem in the neighborhood, as far as anyone could tell. His family is dead. He has no known place of work, which raises a bit of a flag at his age. His phone contact list is virtually nil. It's almost like the man is a ghost."

Stone turns to Baker.

"We know about Ashton's will and that he left everything to you, Claire—"

"Then you should also know I told his attorney yesterday that I have no interest in anything from him."

Mitch puts his beer down. "I was there. The attorney convinced her into mulling over her decision for a few days."

Baker nods and places a trademark toothpick in his mouth. "Claire, could you describe your relationship with the deceased?"

"I didn't have one."

He looks from Claire and Mitch and back again. From the look on Baker's face, he wants more.

"Plain and simple, he was a stalker. By the time I finally learned his name, the only thing I knew was he was a client of Mitch's." She tells them of the time he wore a fake mustache and posed as a building inspector, then their awkward interaction at the Chinese restaurant, and when she accidentally met him at Mitchell's office.

Mitch puts a hand on her arm when he senses her upset grow. He wishes she hadn't told the detectives that he was Ash's therapist, but that cat was out of the bag. Even though his client was dead, Mitch had a duty to keep his professional relationship with Ash confidential, but he believed he could discuss personal aspects of what Ash confided to him about Claire. "Ash admitted he'd somehow been able to obtain a spare key to this place when it was under construction and camped out in the attic, waiting for us." He shows them pictures that he took of the setup Ash had in their attic from his cell phone. "Of course, it's no longer there. He also expressed to me his love for Claire and his desire to replace me. He said when he surreptitiously claimed to have watched us tour this place one night, he said he could have killed me. He also admitted to following us several times before that; exactly when and where I don't know."

Baker turns to Mitch. "You could have told me about this. I could have helped."

"I don't know how you could have helped. He was my client. Several aspects of this are quite spooky in retrospect, but I felt I could handle it. When he admitted what he'd been doing and how he felt about my fiancé, I sent him a certified letter earlier this week informing him I could no longer be his therapist and provided him with a list of other area therapists. He never contacted me about this."

Stone seems excited to at last be hearing something about this mystery man. "What were you seeing him for? Did he ever speak of having enemies?"

Mitch is reluctant to answer and thinks of the picture in Ash's family album. "I don't see the relevance here. No, he did not share with me any realistic proof he had enemies.

Stone speaks up, "Everything you say your client admitted to you, especially his thoughts to kill you, must have been traumatic or, at the very least, terrifying. I can't see a woman committing this crime without help."

There's an awkward lull until Mitch breaks it. "Are you accusing us of killing my client?"

Baker takes the toothpick out of his mouth. "I don't think that's what Detective Stone is saying—"

"He's implying it. This conversation is over."

Stone pushes the chair back and stands. "You two should visit this man's home, especially if you plan to own it. It's a shrine to Claire."

Mitch walks the men to the door and says, "JoJo, thanks for the food. We will have you and Simone over for dinner one day soon.

On his way out, Stone says, "If you think of anything else, I left my card on the kitchen table."

Next Monday, Mitch arranges a walk-through of Ash's house with the estate manager after Baker suggests he do so. There is no crime scene tape at the door, but it feels as if there should be.

When Claire and Mitch enter the second bedroom, she gasps and his attention fixes on the opposite wall. The entire wall is covered with photos, mostly of Claire in various types of casual and formal clothing. Claire at or in her car, outside her apartment, at her work, pics of her music performances, and ones of her singing and playing music through her apartment windows. Some on the periphery include her with Mitch in restaurants or at music venues, and a few are shots of them inside their new home, which include one in which they are having sex.

Then, above his bed in the main bedroom, there are photoshopped pics of Ash and Claire together inside a large heart-shaped drawing. A framed photo of a smiling Claire stands on the nightstand next to his bed.

"This is way past creepy. I have no words to describe this," Claire says to Mitch.

"All I knew was he saw a woman recently he liked and I urged him to introduce himself. I was as shocked as you when I learned the object of his desire was you."

Mitch finds nothing about Ash's family while he searches the house for the family album. He cannot find anything of substance other than a set of nondescript travel books about Hungary and its people.

The next day, Claire and Mitch meet again with Fincher, and she tells him she doesn't want any of Ash's assets.

A month later, a package arrives for Claire at their new house. She opens it and reads the note, which simply says … to Claire, from A.

She looks at the letters and pictures. She doesn't know the significance of the old daguerreotype picture and thinks it strange that the photographer took a picture of an outdoor fire in front of two huts. There's no person in the old sepia picture.

She likes the uniqueness of the old album cover, but she tosses it all in the trash before Mitch gets home from work. She returns to rehearsing the latest song she wrote for her album.

The End

Acknowledgments

I wanted to branch out and write a horror story that could be readily interpreted as something explainable in the real world, so I returned to my clinician character and the multi-dimensional universe of mental illness that he traverses with his clients. In introducing a new love interest for Mitchell, I chose to make her the fulcrum of the story and heighten the stakes that Mitch is unaware of until the denouement. As the tale evolved, it became evident this would be a novella rather than a novel. I learned something about my stories; they reach their conclusions at their own pace and it felt disingenuous to lengthen this to novel size.

I again want to thank my friend Dr. Felix Vincenz for his invaluable expertise in private practice and all things psychiatric. More thanks go to my friend Mike Schaller for his knowledge of the law. I have many great friends. Any mistakes herein are solely mine.

I also want to thank the entire staff at **New York Book Publishers**, especially my two primary project managers, **Lisa "Tokyo" Smith** and **Connor Stewart**. They oversee, format, help create the covers from my ideas, and constantly update my website. Thanks to my main editor **Jeremiah Hofsted**, and other managers **Sarah Parker**, **Tobin Mires**, **Charles Smith**, **Margaret Johnson**, **Emma Becker**, and **Logan Walsh**.